THE
IMMORALS

THEODORE PYSH

Category: Adult
Genre: Literary Fiction, Romance, Crime

Printed in the United States of America

ISBN-13: 978-0-578-81551-0

CHAPTER 1

"Morning After"

E mpty. Hollowed out. Sonya knew that feeling. The morning after the one-night stand. Not that she'd had that many, but it was always the same. Borrowed passion from a transient lover, and then, left alone, as he abruptly goes out into the day. Who was he? Who knows? Maybe Bryan wasn't even his real name. It was easy for men. Not so much for women. At least most women. Men give love for sex. Women give sex for love. Except, of course, the one-night stands. Those are the free for all. Until morning. Then, the woman pays the emotional price of abandonment.

If she's lucky, he sticks around and lets her fix him breakfast so there's some semblance of dignity; maybe an outside chance of a continued relationship. But most often, he escapes the burden of intimacy, taking with him her self-esteem, and all her fantasies of the random knight, rescuing her from the castle tower and the brutal, alcohol induced, sadistic demons of despair who hold her there.

She really just wanted to get out of the apartment for a while. Jenn called at the perfect time. Another boring

Friday evening stuck at home wasn't an inviting idea. Sure! She'd meet for a couple of drinks and the latest gossip. Then these guys show up. Two young women sitting alone in the lounge on a Friday. Irresistible! Sonya tried to decline their obvious moves, but Jennifer was absolutely into it. Surrender! He was good- looking and Sonya had always had a "thing" for a man in a suit. The rest was foggy, but somehow he wound up in her bed. Let the games begin.

Then, it came to her. *"Did he use a condom? Damn it! I had them right there in the drawer! Of course not! He wouldn't care! I haven't renewed my birth control in months. Even worse, what if he had an std? Or Aids? Well, I doubt he had Aids. But I better get to the pharmacy and pick up the Plan B. Fifty bucks later, all sins are forgiven. STD maybe. Pregnancy . . . no way!"*

She wondered how it went for Jenn. Same thing probably. Both those guys were players. But Jenn was different. She enjoyed the game. She was younger than Sonya; twenty something and biting the apple whenever that old tingle came over her. If he was gone in the morning, good riddance. Next! Well, she'd call her later, just to compare notes.

But for now, a mild depression set in. Nothing big. Just a void. An invisible black crow sitting on her shoulder. Two plus years without sex and now this. The last time was with Robert. His idea of foreplay was "oops!" He'd asked her to marry him. *"Not in this life Robert!"*

Robert was the classic retro 1950s' traditionalist. White cottage in the country, with her in continuous barefoot pregnant misery and a slew of screaming kids while

Tarzan Robert brought home the bacon for Sonya Jane and family. At least she dodged that bullet. She'd shake off the depression. Move on. Get down to the pharmacy.

Walgreens was just a walk away from her apartment, so she scurried off to purchase the 'Plan B.'

Back at the apartment she read the instructions and side effects:

Side Effects:
- **Nausea or vomiting**
- **Dizziness**
- **Fatigue**
- **headache**
- **Breast tenderness**
- **Bleeding between periods or heavier menstrual bleeding**
- **Lower abdominal pain or cramps**

"Oh yeah! Now I remember. That's what happened last time. Throwing up, accompanied by a world class headache! Oh well, down the hatch!"

Sonya had never been a big party girl. Her sexual adventures were infrequent. So much so, that she saw no need for birth control pills. But she wasn't a recluse either. A few summers ago, she met a guy at a July 4th get together and one thing led to another. Once again, the condoms (Plan A) never left the bedroom drawer, so it was off to Walgreens for Plan B. These days Sonya was lonely. Now in her 30's the twenty-something parties no longer had the appeal they once had.

She was ready to settle in with a full time, life partner. She would be happy to be monogamous., true and married with children with *'Mister Right.'* Her parents had forever been hinting and hoping for grandchildren. But, she had to get married first. She could never figure out why they named her Sonya. Catholic girls were always named after saints. As far as she knew, there never was a "Saint Sonya" and certainly not a "Saint Sony." Deep down, she hated the name, but then, she didn't get to pick it. She wasn't really close to her parents.

She guessed, being an only child they surely loved her but, it wouldn't have hurt for them to say it once in a while. In all her years, she never heard those words from the lips of either of them. She guessed her father must have wanted a boy. *"What would they have named him? "Sonny?"* At any rate, she wasn't getting any younger; not that 32 was ancient but, looking around, there was no Prince Charming in sight.

"The hell with it! They don't deserve a grandchild!"

With or without Prince Charming, tonight, as like most nights, she'd be wrapped up in her favorite blanket, watching whatever HBO had to offer and blocking out the Catholic guilt of the night before But, she'd wonder: *"Why did he leave so fast today? Out the door at six a.m.! Did I look that bad the morning after? I've heard men talk about "Coyote Ugly" but . . . well, maybe he'll call later. He said he'd call! But they always say they'll call."* Sonya needed closure.

CHAPTER 2

"Bryan"

He drove home in a frenzy. Risking a traffic ticket. He'd had enough of those. He never intended to stay the night. There'd be some explaining to do. The chilly morning air outside made him shiver.

"Damn it! What happened to Global Warming? April, 2018 and it's freezing!"

He wondered if she was up yet. He thought he managed to get out without waking her. He didn't get a good look at her as he quietly exited their bed of harbored lust. *"But she sure looked hot last night at the bar. Then again, they all get better by the beer."* Beer goggles or not, he decided she was a hottie. *"Damn! She had wild green eyes! Said she was a farm girl, grew up in Little Sioux. Ninety-two-miles and a galaxy away from the big city, Omaha, Nebraska."*

What number was she? He'd been with so many. Once, on a road trip from Iowa City to Omaha, he couldn't find anything good on the radio; so, to pass the time, he decided to add up all the women he'd ever been with, losing count at 192. Quick division in his head made that 6 women for every year of his life. Did that make him a sex addict? A womanizer? He worried about that. He hated that word. It sounded so low rent. *"Womanizer! Damn!"* If he were a woman, they'd label him a slut or a nympho or whore. But, looking at it through a man's window, it made him a real stud! He'd prefer that moniker. it was what the shrinks called "sport fucking."

Yeah! He was a stud sportsman! Bryan walked in the shallows of emotion. His couldn't let himself out into the deep, outer waters where he might swim into a wave of painful heartbreak. Things were just fine here in the ankle deep. He didn't lose his virginity until he was 18 and the girl who took him there broke his heart. Once burned, twice shy. He wasn't going to risk loving someone again. He'd go through the motions and pretend for a while, both to himself and whomever he was playing with this time. But his heart wasn't going out for a ride like that first one any time soon.

Anyway, in the advertising business, everyone was screwing with everyone else all the time. Especially if you were on the road. And that he was. Mr. Robbins had "*A woman in every port*" as the saying goes. Anyway, it was a wild night and he got to run his numbers and she got to pretend he seduced her. It was immediately clear to Bryan Robbins she didn't go there just to meet friends and have a few drinks.

And so, as far as he was concerned, they both got what they were looking for. No strings, no harm, no foul, no condom. He never used a condom no matter the sex partner; except for the time he went to the "Moonlight

Bunny Ranch" in Carson City. They made you use condoms there. But other than that; fat, skinny, white, black or in between, he didn't like the synthetic feeling of condoms, and he was willing to trade the chance of contracting something in exchange for a more pleasurable experience. Thirty-seven-years old and 192 spins of the big venereal disease wheel later, he was still pristine clean. *"Was that just blind luck?"* Had to be.

He might call her later just to connect and apologize for leaving so early. Had to show some empathy. She was pretty good in bed and he knew a little contrived caring would go a long way to another round sometime down the road.

CHAPTER 3

"Sunday Morning"

"Well, he's not gonna call"

Sonya kept the phone close to her all-day Saturday, telling herself he'd call; but knowing full well it wasn't going to happen. She even went to bed later than usual just in case. It wasn't that he was any kind of special, she just needed the cleansing a phone call would do for her soul and self- image.

The morning came quickly, and she found herself sitting at the kitchen table just staring at the phone like a lonely child stares out the window waiting for dad to return home from a business trip. *"Call me Damn it!"* She felt so foolish. Might as well get up and get the paper outside the door and go through her regular Sunday routine: Toasted English muffin, two pop tarts, coffee, orange juice and the Sunday news. It wasn't that she didn't know how to cook. Farm girls were scrambling eggs by the third grade. But since graduating from college in Omaha, Sonya had morphed into a city girl, and it wasn't much fun just cooking for herself.

She had barely bitten into the first pop tart when the headline article almost made her knock over the coffee.

Local Man Found Dead in Bar Restroom!
(Police suspect foul play)

Omaha police Friday night discovered a white male individual dead at the Interlude Lounge, 74th and Pacific Street, after a bar patron called 911 to report a man lying face down on the floor of a toilet stall inside the restroom. The victim's name was being held pending notification of kin, but several lounge patrons identified the man as Jerry Coliano, a well-known local businessman, thought to have ties to organized crime No suspects have been identified, but authorities describe the fatality as a "mob like" homicide.

"Holy crap! The Interlude! That's where we met those guys!

And then, the phone rang.

"It's him!"

But it wasn't.

"Sony! Hi! It's me!"

"Hi Jenn! I meant to call you yesterday. Have you seen the paper?"

"You know it girlfriend! That's why I called you! Can you believe this? Right where we were! It'll be a cold day in Hell before we go back there again. Whew!"

"I know! This is like a bad movie! I didn't know that Coliano guy frequented the Interlude. This is bizarre! Well, let's talk later, I'm gonna read the rest of the article. You can tell me all about how things went for you Friday night."

Shootings and murders weren't an uncommon thing in Omaha, Nebraska. People on the coasts think of it as some small burg in the middle of nothing, where the settlers still fight Indians and have a pony express station; when in fact, the metropolitan area population is more than a million souls. And, while shootings and homicides average almost one a week, they're primarily on the North side of the city where the gangs' rule. This kind of thing was a rare occurrence out in the West side of town.

Sonya was both unnerved and fascinated by the incident. Knowing she was that close to it both scared and excited her.

"I wonder if it happened while I was still there. Maybe the killer was there when we were, sitting close to us. What does a murderer look like? Hell, how would I know?" Everybody in town knew that Coliano guy. He was Omaha's version of Tony Soprano. But I never saw him in the bar. He must have come later"

And so, for Sonya, the dull, calm, relaxing Sunday morning breakfast, became an adrenaline rush of excitement, fear and fantasy. She did get a phone call, but not the one she was hoping for.

Just then, it rang again.

CHAPTER 4

"Glad I ran into you!"

"Hello!"

"Hi! Is this Sonya?"

It was him. *"Took him long enough"*

"Yes! This is Sonya! Who's this?"

Of course, she knew, but she had to be coy.

"This is Bryan! I'm just calling to apologize for leaving so abruptly the other day"

Still trying to sound like she didn't care. Sonya gathered the most apathetic voice she could muster.

"Well, that's ok. What happened?"

"My dogs! I hadn't let them out all night! When I woke up yesterday morning it hit me! If I didn't get home quick, they'd go all over the carpeting. I'm so sorry. You looked so peaceful there in bed, I didn't want to wake you. Anyway, I hope you understand. I just called to apologize, and I hope I can see you again sometime soon. It was a terrific evening."

Now the ball was in his court.

"Well, I appreciate the apology Bryan. I'd like to see you again."

"Perfect! Thank you Sonya! By the way, did you see that Coliano guy got murdered at the bar that night?"

"Yes! I just read about it! That's wild huh?"

"Yeah, same place we met! Ok, well, if it's ok with you, I'll give you a call this week and we can meet for dinner or drinks or something.

"That'll be fine Bryan. And thanks for the phone call."

"No worries! I'll be touch. Bye now!"

This was good. He finally called. Her self-image somewhat restored, Sonya decided to venture out and fill up the car. It was almost on empty and she had work in the morning. Might as well fill it up now. Nothing else to do.

Her white, 2018 Toyota Camry was parked in the apartment complex parking lot. She could have rented one of the garages for $40 a month but opted out. Almost every day during the winter she wound up wishing she'd spent the extra money as she brushed snow off the hood and chipped ice from the windshield with a credit card. But then, soon enough, the warmth of spring came, and the garage seemed un-necessary.

Her car came brand new, with just 8 brand spanking new miles on the odometer. It was more than she could afford, but she fell in love. Like all automobile manufacturers, the color wasn't Just "white" Toyota's name was: *Wind Chill Pearl*, with supple, spade black heated seats. JBL stereo system, and all the other toys.

"Anyway, I'll probably get a raise soon and that'll help make the payments. Besides! New car warranty, so I'll save on repairs! It'll all come out in the wash. Don't I deserve to have a new car?"

She started the car, out onto the street in search of petrol. With that, Sonya's cell phone fell on the floor by the brake pedal.

"Damnit"

She tries to scrape it back toward her with her foot, but it's not budging. Frustrated, she leans down for just a moment and . . . BAM!

"Oh no! Please God no! Not today! My beautiful car!"

Sonya had rear ended the Subaru in front of her. Wasn't a big slam, but cars these days take big damage with even minor bumps. Now, the world around her was a deafening circus. People honking in all directions, laying on their horns and yelling obscenities for her and the recipient of her mishap to get out of the way. That was easier said than done. Two lane road, steam's coming out of her loving Toyota's now smashed in hood.

In the midst of the chaos, the Subaru's door opens out into the noise and a man emerges, slowly, calmly and without any sign of irritation he walks towards Sonya, still sitting in the Toyota, crying in fear and desperation, anticipating what was to come next.

As he approached, even with her anxiety and clouded vision, she was taken aback by his strong, silent, unprovoked presence. He was every kind of handsome. Pick your type. He was that type. A shade over six feet. Maybe mid 30's, black, camel hair sport coat with a deep Navy "T" underneath, stretched tight enough to accentuate a six-pack stomach; just like the guys you see on those exercise commercials on TV. It all topped off with Dean Martin like curled hair, black as a starless night, and azure, blue eyes, impossibly hypnotic.

"Are you alright miss?"

"Oh my God! I am so sorry! I dropped my phone and then..."

"Whoa! It's ok! It happens! Let's see if we can get our vehicles on the side of the road"

With that, the man removed his camel hair coat, revealing his entire Adonis physique and pulled up on the Toyota's front bumper to unhitch it from his. With that he motioned for Sonya to put the car in neutral and turn toward the curb. Then he got behind her car and pushed it to the side.

Then, jumping to his Subaru, which was still drivable, he diverted his to the curb right in front of her. All the noise subsided as cars passed them, now busily on their way to their destinations.

By this time, Sonya was simply bawling. She reached over and pulled her insurance card out of the glove box.

"Oh God! Did I pay my insurance? Please God, say I paid my insurance!"

Once again, he approached her and bent down on her driver's side to speak.

"I know! I know! It was my fault sir! I rear ended you! Are you going to call the police?"

"I don't see any need for that Miss. Why don't we just get our own vehicles fixed and we'll leave it at that. I think you're shook up enough. I just want to know if you're alright. Do you need me to get you to the ER?"

"What! How can this be? He's going to just let it go?"

"Well, no! I'm fine sir. Or, at least I think I am. I haven't gotten out of the car since I hit you!"

"Well, let's start with that."

He opened her door, and Sonya clumsily slid out and stood on the pavement. The wind from the passing vehicles blowing her hair into a jumbled mess.

"How do you feel? Are you alright?

"I'm ok! Better than I look I'm sure!"

"Damn! Why didn't I put some make up on before I left the apartment? All this crying. I must look awful!"

"Listen, let me call a tow company for your car and then I'll take you home or wherever you were heading."

"You don't have to do that; I have a friend who can pick me up!"

"What friend am I thinking of? I have no friends!"

"Nonsense! In fact, let's drive over to that coffee shop up the block and we can both calm down while you wait for the tow truck."

For Sonya, this was a kiss from heaven. Of course, she would love that.

"Alright sir, at this point, I guess that's a good idea. You sure you won't be embarrassed to be seen with me dressed like this with crying eyes?"

"You look fine, and by the way, my name is Tony"

"Hello Tony, my name is Sonya, but people call me Sony"

"Of course, his name is Tony. What else would it be? God never made a bad looking Tony."

The man walked her over to the passenger side of his Subaru and opened the door for her. She remembered reading: "When a man opens the car door for a woman, it's either a new car or a new wife." Not this time.

Once in the coffee shop, Tony pulled out a chair for her right by a window so Sonya could see her banged up Toyota just a block away, waiting patiently for the tow truck to arrive. But Sonya wasn't in a hurry anyway. She could have sat with Mr. Dreamy, drinking coffee forever.

He came back from the counter with a Carmel Latte' and croissant for Sonya and a black coffee for himself.

"Here you are young lady!"

"Thank you, sir, err . . . Tony! But how did you know . . .?"

"I just guessed. So, I did ok?"

"You did perfect! And thank you again! But, am I holding you up? Weren't you on your way to "work?"

"No. Actually, I was heading back home to Kansas City. I had some business here last week. It lasted into the weekend".

"Oh? What kind of business are you in?"

"I'm a contractor of sorts."

"You mean like a building contractor?"

"Something like that. I'm a consultant. Free agent. What do you do?"

"I'm an administrative assistant to a packaging company Vice President."

"There's the tow truck! I told them to take your car to the Toyota Dealership with the sticker on your license plate. Is that ok?"

"Well yes! You're very observant! But I better get going. See if I can get a ride with them."

"Don't worry about it. Finish your Latte'. I'll give you a ride home and you can call the insurance company."

"You don't have to do that Mr . . ."

"Sanders! Tony Sanders!" And It would be my pleasure to drive you home."

This was getting too good to be true. Sonya abandoned any fear that her newfound friend might be a rapist or criminal of some sort.

"Maybe he's a serial killer! But, what a way to go!"

"Alright then, but I don't know how to thank you."

"No need! I'll just drop you off at your home and be on my way. I'm guessing you don't live very far from here?"

"No, it's an apartment complex just a couple of miles from here."

"Alright then! Ready to go?"

"Sure! And thank you so much!"

Walking out to the parking lot in front of the coffee shop, Sonya then noticed Tony's car had a Missouri license plate. But a pale green Subaru Outback just didn't seem to fit his persona. She would have figured him for some kind of sports car. Maybe a Camaro or even a Vette but a Subaru just didn't seem right.

"Maybe he's married with a pile of kids? Probably has a drop-dead gorgeous wife who makes love to him twenty times a day. I know I would."

On the way to her apartment, Sonya was quick to keep the conversation going.

"So, do you have a lot of children Tony?"

"Actually, I don't have any. I've never been married. Too busy I guess"

"Never been married! Oh God! I need to figure something out quick."

"There it is, my apartment complex! Just turn right at the next red light. Listen, I'm going to give you my phone number and insurance information, just in case you change your mind about the accident. It was my fault!"

"Really Sonya, don't worry about it. I'll take care of it. But, if it's ok, I'd be happy to have your phone number. I'll give you mine if you want. If it's ok, I'll call next time I'm in town or vice versa and maybe we can have dinner or something. Would that be ok?"

"Would that be ok? Yes! That would be beyond ok! And guess what! There is a God!"

"I would love that! Here's my number! Please call me anytime, and please text me your number, I don't know how to thank you. Really. This has been wonderful. You've been wonderful!"

"Well, have a good day Sonya. I hope I'll see you again real soon."

Sonya watched him drive away and kept looking until his car was completely out of sight. Then she slowly turned and levitated towards her apartment door.

"I believe in Santa Claus, the Easter Bunny, Cupid, and Sir Galahad! I know that because he just left

In this moment, Sonya didn't even care about her car wreck. In fact, she was glad it happened. She'd have an accident on purpose if she knew there'd be a Tony on the other end of a smashed bumper. Then, her phone did the familiar "ding" of someone texting and there it was, Mr. Tony Sander's number.

CHAPTER 5

"The Name Game"

T he drive from Omaha to Kansas City is about three-and-a- half hours on Interstate 29 South.

For most of the drive back home, Tony thought about this new lady he met. That Sonya was a beauty. Maybe five- foot- six, eyes like green emeralds, damn near perfect figure. Still she wasn't full of herself. Had that 'girl next door look' and demeanor. He wanted to call her on the drive down but decided against it. Might be too presumptive.

"I should have told her my real last name. Wouldn't have hurt anything. Still, better to err on the side of caution. Anyway, If I see her again, I'll tell her. Who knows? Meanwhile, I'm not turning this rental car into insurance. Looks like about $2500 damage. At least it's drivable. But that cuts deep into my contract profits. $5000 for the deal, minus hotel, gas and expenses. I'll be lucky to net $1500 bucks! Ahh well! There'll be other jobs."

After the long drive, Tony pulled into the airport rental center with the crippled vehicle. There no way to camouflage the damage, and the lot attendant came out to the car half running.

"Damn Mr. Sanders! What happened?"

"I got rear ended by a woman"

"Wow! Did you get her insurance information?"

"No, she didn't have insurance" (A little white lie but it didn't matter)

"Well, Sir, it looks like quite a fender bender! How do you want to handle this?"

"Tell you what. You have all my contact and credit card information. I don't want to turn it into insurance. My rates will just go up. But don't charge it to my credit card. Just get an estimate and I'll pay you cash for the rental and damages. Will that work?"

"Sure Mr. Sanders, that will be fine."

"Ok! I'm going to call UBER and get home. I have a meeting this afternoon."

Being an extremely private individual, Tony never used his legal name when he traveled. As far as the rental company, hotels and Sonya Hartiq were concerned, his last name was Sanders. He had drivers licenses, credit cards, and even passports for both Mr. Anthony Sanders and Messina, and even a couple others. One of the advantages of knowing somebody in the forgery business.

Tony Messina was a private contractor but, everybody answers to somebody. Like most private enterprises, Tony answered to his clients. For this Omaha project, it was Julian "The Machete" Infantino. This guy pretty much ran the whole city. You needed something? Primo tickets to the Chief's games? A speeding ticket fixed? Whatever it was, he'd get it for you if he liked you or you were connected.

One could only guess why they called him "The Machete" but it surely wasn't meant as a term of endearment. He somehow earned the moniker back in the day as he was 'coming up' in the ranks with Tony's father.

Tony's dad worked together with Julian back in the late 80's. Sometimes Tony's dad would bring him to work when they'd meet up. To Tony, he was "Mr. Infantino." He was like family. When Tony was just 27, his dad passed away suddenly from a heart attack. At the time, Tony was working construction, but soon after his father's passing he came to Mr. Infantino to ask for work in his operation.

He kept hanging around until Julian finally gave in and got Tony some contracting work. He was good at it. It didn't take long before he was making serious money and even passing up contracts he didn't like. He would follow in his father's footsteps.

Today, as he arrived back in Kansas City, he made a beeline for Jules Infantino's headquarters. It was simply a bar called Uncle Jimmy's in downtown. Built in the 1940's, it showed its age. The wooden floors creaked all the way down to the end of the bar where Jules Infantino sat holding court at a table with all of his cronies.

"Well, I'm back Mr. Infantino"

Tony could never bring himself to call him Julian or Jules. He was a man 37 years old and, it always sounded funny to the others sitting around the table. Tony was a kind of badass, known for having a short fuse. They all HEARD the story where he had beaten up a dude in a bar fight over a Ten-dollar pool game. He poked an eyeball out with a pool cue and the cops literally had to pull him off the guy. Julian Infantino came to the rescue there as well. Tony was arrested but, bailed out an hour later and the other guy never pressed charges for his lost eyesight. There were other stories too. He wasn't one you wanted to scramble with. Yet, when he spoke to Julian Infantino, it was with the utmost respect and affection. For his part, "Mr. Infantino" liked it very much.

"Tony my boy! Welcome back! I heard things went well in Omaha! The client's very happy!"

"That's good to know Mr. Infantino! I did my best.

"Sit down! Have a drink! Sammy! Get my boy Tony here a drink!"

"It's alright sir, I really have to go. I just wanted to check in with you to make sure everybody was satisfied with my work."

"They said you did a very professional job son! No worries! You take care of yourself, hear me? We'll find you some more work soon."

"Yes sir! Thank you so much! Have a good day!"

Tony wanted to get back to his apartment and somehow contact with Sonya. He'd known a lot of women, and maybe the special thing about her was just that she was new, maybe his infatuation with her would wear off. But, he needed to find out just what it was that kept her invading his thoughts.

CHAPTER 6

"Breaking up is hard to do!"

Monday morning came fast. Sonya walked into work right on time without a minute to spare. *"Safe!"* No "You're late again!" lectures for her *this* time. But she hated the job. The world's greatest container company. You need a container? Any kind, any size, any this, any that, and *"Container City"* has what you're looking for. Their mantra was: **"Container City, Boxing Champions of the World!"** Sonya had the dream job. Her boss was a short, fat, bald, middle aged, empty suit pervert with dirty fingernails, who had no idea just how stupid, homely and incompetent he was. Google the words "ugly, sloppy pig" and there's his picture. Robert (Bobby) Bosse' oversaw Container Distribution, and Sonya was his administrative assistant.

Like most working relationships of the kind, she did the work and he got the "wonderful." Standing up there at the Christmas party, getting his "Atta Boy" plaque and a big check. Everyone applauded. For her part, Sonya got $37k a year, no raises in forever, and a Honey Baked Ham Christmas bonus.

"Ahh well" She liked ham

But this had to stop. She'd put her resume' on 3 different job web sites to no avail.

"Bachelor's degree in Fine Arts. That and $6.50 will get you a latte at Starbucks. Today, if it's not some kind of computer science thing, you might as well not even go to college."

And so, the day dragged on. It was hard not to be a clock watcher, and the old cliché' *'A watched pot never boils'* definitely applied.

"Thirty-five more minutes and Monday is over!"

Sonya couldn't wait.

And then, Mr. Bosse' came out to visit.

"Uh, Sonya, could you please come into my office for a bit?"

"Sure Mr. Bosse'! Is something wrong?"

"We just need to talk."

"Can I grab some coffee?"

"Uh ... no, just please come on in."

This couldn't be good. Sonya set her laptop down and walked into Robert (Bobby) Bosse's office with justified anticipation.

Opening his office door, the pungent smell of body odor invaded her nostrils. The walls of his office were permeated with an odious repugnancy of an occupant who continually ignored his own personal hygiene; making whomever entered a prisoner of olfactory pain.

His desk mirrored his filthy lifestyle. Half eaten lunches from long ago intermingled themselves with stacks of papers stained with the offspring of the lunches' goo.

And on the perfunctory tie he wore as Container Distribution Manager was a souvenir of today's Thai food lunch catastrophe.

"Shut the door behind you please Sonya!"

"Uh . . . alright! How can I help you sir?"

She hated calling him sir.

"Well, Sonya. We have a problem. As you know, the bar has been set high for Container City's employee standards.

"Really? What standards could this slob possibly be talking about?"

"Yes sir, I know that sir."

"Well, unfortunately Sonya, your work ethic and performance has not lived up to company expectations. As my administrative assistant, I need more commitment to the position."

"Ok! So . . . you need me to do better?"

"Actually Sonya, we're going to have to let you go."

"Let me go? You mean you're firing me?"

"I'm afraid so."

"Mr. Bosse' please don't do this! I'll do better! I promise!"

"I'm sorry, Sonya. We've already hired your replacement.

Those words pushed a button on Sonya she never realized was there. She fired off at him.

"Mr. Bosse', I mean BOBBY! You are the most insensitive, disgusting, incompetent, hygienically challenged, filthy pig I have come across in my entire life! I can't even believe you would do this to me! When you say I act like I'm not committed . . . I'm not acting! Kiss off fat man!"

"Ok, that's enough! Pack up your personal belongings It's time for you to leave! Security will escort you out of the building. You have ten minutes."

The humiliation of being escorted out was almost unbearable. Everyone staring at her as she exited the office. They knew what happened. Down the elevator to the first floor, past the security guards standing lazily at the front desk soliciting her for her employee work badge as she left through the revolving doors. Sonya always hoped that she would be the one to give notice. Not this way. How could the higher ups not see what a joke this guy was?

"At least I got to tell that asshole how I felt about him. But what if my outburst causes them to give me a bad recommendation or Blacklist me or something? Ahh, I don't care. It was worth it. I hope. I've got to find another job pronto! I need a drink!

And as if summoned by some Magical Genie, the cell phone rang.

"Hey Sony! It's me again! Welcome to the week girlfriend! Want to go out? Those guys we met over the weekend want to meet us again.

"Well, that was quick!"

"I don't know Jenn. I'm up for a couple of drinks but, I'm not sure I want to party. It's only Monday!"

Sonya knew how the night would end up.

"Aww! C'mon girlfriend! It'll be fun!"

"Let me think about it, I'll call you back in a bit. I've had a rough day."

"All the more reason to go!"

"I'II call you back!.

What Sonya really hoped for was a call from Tony Sanders. A weekend invitation.

"He's probably forgotten about me altogether. A man like that probably has a stable of women to choose from. Plus, he's from Kansas City, long distance relationships never work out"

But, as the day moved along, the thought of another encounter with Bryan sounded more and more inviting. Not what a good Catholic farm girl from Little Sioux Iowa should be thinking about, but she'd morphed into a city woman long ago. It would be a perfect distraction from the brutal day she just experienced. She would go again tonight and see what it brings.

CHAPTER 7

"Burning Love!"

S oon after she hung up with Jennifer, Sonya felt a twitch. Maybe not really a *"twitch,"* more like a *burn*; but not really a burn either, right down in the last place you would want it to be. *"For God's sake, what's this about?"*

What it was about was about 72 hours. Seventy- two hours ago our girl had unprotected sex with a stranger. And the price Sonya *thought* she paid was just a down stroke. ***"COME on!"*** Sonya knew damn well what it was, but she didn't want to believe it. She'd never had one before, but she knew well the symptoms of an STD. *"Probably more of those Plan B effects! Uh huh. Sure Sony, that's what it is!"*

She didn't bother to call Jennifer back. She'd not be going out.

As the night wore on, things seemed pretty much ok. But Sonya was afraid to go to the bathroom. *"I'll just hold it, I don't really have to go yet"* But right before bed, the crowd got ugly. She had to go so badly, she broke the seal and let it flow.

It wasn't a "tingle" anymore. It was a flaming hot urine holocaust. Sonya almost let out a scream of pain but held it back. This was an apartment building and the walls weren't that well insulated. Sonya finished the painful experience, wiped off, and decided she'd call her gynecologist in the morning.

Morning came all too fast. Time to pee again. *"Oh God! Alright, let's get it over with"*

Sonya peed. It hurt. But not as bad as last night. *"Maybe it isn't what I thought!"*

"Fat chance Sony. Call the Doctor."

She did.

"Good morning! Doctor Raymond's office. How can I help you?"

"Uh, this is Sonya Hartiq, I'd like to make an appointment with Doctor Raymond."

"Ok, what's the problem, Ms. Hartiq?"

"Uh... I think I may have a yeast infection or something"

"Ok! Well, I have a cancellation at 2 p.m. today. Can you come in then?"

"I'll make it work! Thank you!"

* * *

No sooner had she arrived in the doctor's lobby and the nurse opened the door.

"Sonya Hartiq?"

"Yes, that's me!"

"Please come on back!"

Sonya was happy to be seen so soon by the doctor. At least something was going right today.

"Hi! Do they call you Sonya?"

"Sonya, Sony, either one is ok"

"Ok Sonya let's get your weight. Want to take off your shoes?"

"Uh..no . . . that's ok. Let's just do it."

"Ok . . . please step on the scale. 128! not bad young lady!"

Sonya was just 5' 5", 128, perfectly height, weight proportionate. She just wished her breasts were a little bigger. She was a "C" cup. Perfect by most measures, but almost all women feel their breasts are inadequate; too big, too small, too something.

"I need you to urinate in this cup Sonya. When you're finished, just set it inside that little door. Then, if you will, please strip down and put this gown on, the doctor will see you in just a bit"

"Just a bit" turned out to be almost twenty minutes. Sony was getting irritated and concerned.

A small knock on the exam room door.

"Hello Sonya! It's good to see you again! Sorry for the wait. This is nurse Samuelson. Let's get you up on the table and see what's going on. Feet in the stirrups please!"

Sonya knew this part all too well. The cold metal of the stirrups on her feet ran a slight shiver up her spine. She felt so vulnerable. She'd been going to Doctor Raymond for almost three years. She thought he was a good doctor, but it was always awkward. The doctor, head poking up from under Sonya's hospital gown said "Hmmm" in the intimidating way that doctors sometimes do.

"What the hell does THAT mean?"

"Well, Sonya, I have good news and bad news. I have to ask you, have you been sexually active lately?"

"Oh No! Now what?"

"Uh, not very much. I don't remember the last time actually." This was embarrassing.

"Well, I hope you can refresh your memory. "Ms. Hartiq, you have somehow contracted gonorrhea and possibly chlamydia. The good news is, we can fix it."

"You mean both? Oh my God! How do you fix it? You mean cure it?"

"Well, yes. Hopefully. Some strains are resistant to antibiotics, but 10 days on these should give you curative relief. I'm going to write you a prescription for ceftriaxone and doxycycline. Those should take care of the problem. Meanwhile, we need to report this to the department of Health and Human Services. I'LL need the names and contact information of anyone you've had sex with in the last six months."

"Well, why would you need that doctor? You don't need to contact the Health Department! I haven't had sex with anyone in forever"

"I'm afraid it's the law Sonya. I have to report this to the State. You must have had sexual relations with someone in the recent past. You don't get gonorrhea from toilet seats. We should get some blood too, check for HIV."

"Well, there was one man, but ... Please don't report this!"

Things were getting very tense. The nurse tried to pretend she wasn't even in the room. In fact, she slowly edged herself toward the exam room door. Shedidn't want to be there for that part of the conversation.

"Ms. Hartiq!" Now he was being formal! No more first name basis. This wasn't open for debate. "I have to report this, and I have to have his name. I could lose my license if I concealed this diagnosis."

Somehow, the nurse got to the door, opened it slowly and sneaked out of the room.!

Of course, Sonya didn't know Bryan's last name. How does she tell that to the doctor? how to say she didn't know his last name? Even today, society has a name for women who have sex with strangers.

"Well, ok doctor. I'm not sure what his name is. We dated a couple of times, and I think he gave me a fake name. He said it was Bryan Crosby. We never went to his home. After a couple of weeks, he just disappeared."

"Ms. Hartiq", (There was that "Ms. Hartiq" again. He meant business)

"I'll forward this information to HHS. Be prepared for them to do a follow up interview with you. This guy could be spreading this all over the city"

CHAPTER 8

"Missed you!"

"Hello Girlfriend! We missed you last night!"

"I know Jenn, I should have called you. I just wasn't feeling well. It came over me in a flash"

"It's ok! It's probably just as well you didn't make it anyway. That Bryan dude showed up looking around for you but, off to the side, you remember, the other guy, Stan? He told me that Bryan is married with two kids. Did he tell you that last weekend?"

"No, he didn't mention that at all. Is that Stan guy married too?"

"No! He's cool! Divorced, no kids, just didn't work out I guess."

"Say Jenn! Did you happen to get Bryan's last name?"

"Uh ... yeah! It's Robbins. Bryan Robbins! He's an account executive at a local advertising agency.

He and Stan work together. He told me the name of the place but, I don't remember what it was."

That was good information for Sonya. She didn't want to appear too interested. She wasn't

going to tell Jennifer all the facts. *"A secret kept is your slave, a secret told is your master."* She just lost

her job and, had plenty of time to Google local advertising agencies and keep calling them all until she

found the one where he worked. She'd confront him about the STD souvenir he left her.

It had to be him. She hadn't had sex with anyone else in almost two years and as the doctor said: "You don't get gonorrhea from toilet seats."

Then she thought:

"But he's married! Doesn't he have sex with his wife? Maybe she's a player too! Maybe she's the one who gave it to him! I don't know, but I'm gonna find out!"

It didn't take her long to find him.

"Good morning! TDS advertising! How may I direct your call?"

"Hello, is Bryan Robbins available this morning?"

"One moment please!"

Bingo! Four random calls to Omaha Ad agencies and she hit the mark!

"Hello! Bryan Robbins here, how can I help you?"

"Hi Bryan! This is Sonya! Remember me?"

"Sonya! Absolutely! How have you been? I was hoping I'd see you the other night, but you never showed. What's up?"

Bryan's surprised, happy response to hear from her threw Sonya's demeanor off somewhat.

"Uh ... Bryan, I'm calling because when we were together last weekend, you left me a little gift."

"Oh! What kind of gift?"

She made the statement in the sternest voice she could muster.

"You gave me an STD Bryan!"

"What? An STD! That's impossible!"

"Gonorrhea Bryan! My doctor didn't think it was impossible! And I haven't had sex with anyone but you in almost two years."

"Listen Sonya. You've got this all wrong! I don't have gonorrhea or anything else like that. If you have an STD you got it from somewhere else. Maybe a toilet seat! I don't know! But not ME!

As it turned out, Bryan in fact, *did* have gonorrhea but, like many others, he was asymptomatic. He had no idea.

"I got it from you Bryan and you better see your doctor and while you're at it, tell your wife about it too!"

"My wife! How did she know about my wife?"

"I've gotta go. You are one crazy bitch!"

With that, Bryan Robbins hung up the phone.

For her part, Sonya didn't know what to do next.

"Should I call the Doctor and give him Bryan's name and contact information? Or, should I let this take its course? I've got the medication "I" need. I don't want any more attention. Let him fall in his own wells. I told him about it. If he wants to infect his family, I guess that's his business. I'm done worrying about other people's problems. I have my own."

That she did. Sonya was reminded that she was now unemployed. They didn't even give her severance. She could file for unemployment, but that would only cover a small portion of her bills. She needed a job.

Now that the confrontation with Mr. Robbins was complete, she had plenty of time to update her resume' and put it out online. The job market was good in Omaha. Surely somebody would be interested.

CHAPTER 9

"Call me Sony!"

T wo weeks had gone by since the accident. The damage to her Toyota was $2762. Fortunately, Sonya had only a $500 deductible. Since Tony didn't turn his car into insurance, Sonya got away with telling a little white lie:

"Somebody backed into my car in the parking lot. It was a hit and run!"

And so, Sonya got her vehicle back. She would still have to pay the deductible, but, because it was a "no fault" accident, at least her insurance rates wouldn't go up. $500 right now was a tough number to come up with, being unemployed and all. She had $1100 saved at the credit union where she got her car loan, but that wouldn't last long even without the $500 she had to pay.

* * *

The state unemployment office was standard government issue. A sterile building inside and out. There were two very bored looking policemen, one sitting next to the front entrance and one at the exit door. To Sonya, it looked like there were a thousand people waiting in line. Mothers, most of whom looked to be Hispanic, with children hanging on their skirts. Unshaven men who seemed to be in the construction trade, with their work boots on, ready to go at the first word of a job opening.

Others, you could tell were just there going through the motions. Probably didn't even want a job but had to report once a week to tell the counselor about all the interviews they'd had. The not so secret, secret was that everyone knew they never really went for job interviews. They'd just make places up and write them out on the sheet. The counselors didn't have the time or the inclination to investigate the validity of what they had written down.

Sonya took a number. She was number 94. Just then a voice came over the speaker in the ceiling.

"Now serving number 67 at window 12"

"67! I'm number 94! That's seventeen numbers! What time is it? What time do they close?"

"Pardon me officer! What time does this office close?"

"4:30 p.m. sharp ma'am'!"

"Well, it's 2:20 now! I'm number 94! What happens if they don't get to my number before closing time?

"I wouldn't worry about it lady. They've got this thing down to a science. They stop taking numbers at 3 p.m. You've got a little wait, but they'll get to you."

"Oh! Thank God!"

"Yeah, just take a seat if you can find one. Like I said, they'll get to you"

Things actually went by somewhat faster than Sonya imagined they would. She'd been there just twenty-five or thirty minutes and they were *"Now serving number 79!"* And, in fact, she found an empty seat. It wouldn't be much longer.

It was almost exactly 3:30 p.m. when she got the call: "Now serving number 94 at window 14"

"Yes!"

She'd been playing *"Candy Crush"* on her mobile phone while she waited, not even paying attention to the clock, and now they called her number. It was like being called to the stage on 'The Price is Right!'

"Sonya Hartiq! Come on down!"

Sonya scurried like a rabbit to window 14, lest they call someone else to take window 14's place. And there, on the other side of what she assumed was bullet proof glass, sat her unemployment salvation. The plastic name tag on his blue, J.C. Penney dress shirt said **Mr. Calvin Stefanski.** *Right away, Sonya could tell that Calvin was the guy who got picked on in high school. This wasn't his first day wearing that shirt either, and the cheap brown and green striped tie didn't match its blue color.*

About mid fifty's Calvin had a few wisps of hair left on his pointed skull, which he combed over with some kind of Dollar Store pure grease hair ointment that made sure the strips of hair laid flat and oily across his barren scalp.

"Good afternoon miss! How can I help you?"

"Well sir, I was laid off from Container City about two weeks ago, and I need to file for unemployment."

"Alright! What's your name little lady?"

"Little lady? Is that how they train these guys to talk?"

But, Sonya wasn't going to push it. Calvin Stefanski was the gatekeeper to her unemployment check.

"My name is Sonya J. Hartiq sir"

"Date of birth?"

"November 13, 1981"

"And your Social Security Number"

"It's right here on the sheet I filled out sir"

"Ahh yes! Here it is! Well, Sweetheart, it seems we have a problem here."

"Sweetheart? He's calling me Sweetheart?"

"What do you mean, problem?"

"Well, seems you were an administrative assistant to a Mr. Bosse', is that correct?"

"Well, yes."

"Apparently Mr. Bosse' fired you for "Cause!"

"For Cause? What does that mean?"

"It means you did something wrong. Maybe violated the company policy manual or were insubordinate or something like that"

"Why, that's just not true. There must be some mistake!"

"that's what your employer wrote in your termination papers. And if you were terminated "For Cause" you're not eligible for unemployment compensation."

Now Sonya knew why there was bullet proof glass between them. If she'd had a gun...

"Please sir! I need this money!"

Out of my hands Sweetheart! But, if you want, you can appeal their termination statement. You can acquire a hearing from a neutral judge. Would you like an appeal application?

Now, on the brink of desperation tears, Sonya swallowed hard and somehow spoke in a broken voice:

"Yes, Please."

Calvin Stefanski handed Sonya the document through the slit at the bottom of the glass and abruptly announced on his microphone:

"Now Serving number 102 at window 14"

Sonya stood up off her chair, tears welling in her eyes and half walked, half ran out of the employment office. It seemed like an hour to navigate the few steps to her car in the parking lot. She fumbled for her keys. Of course, they found their way to the very bottom of her purse. Once inside Sonya began bawling uncontrollably.

Just then, her cell phone rang.

"Hu... hullo?"

"Hi! Is this Sonya?"

Sonya gathered her voice together:

"Uh Yes!"

"Sonya! This is Tony Sanders, Remember me?"

Sonya's composure was coming back, now she'd be coy.

"Hmmm... yes! Tony! You're the gentleman I ran into! How are you?"

"Well, I'm fine Sonya are YOU ok?"

"Yes sir! My car is fixed. I'm doing well."

"That's terrific! Listen, Lady Gaga's performing here in Kansas City this weekend. I have magnificent seats! I was wondering if you wanted to join me for the concert?"

"She had no money, but she'd beg borrow or steal it to get to him. Still, she had to be coy"

"Well, Tony I'd love to, but I'm a little short on cash right now."

"I'm not asking you to pay for the tickets Sonya, I just want to see you again. If you can get down here, we'll go out for dinner, take in the concert, and I'll get you a room at the Rafael down on the plaza. You'll be back home by Sunday afternoon!"

"This can't be real!"

"Oh Tony, I couldn't ask you to do that!"

"You're not asking. I'm asking! I'd like to get to know you better Sonya. I promise you'll have a wonderful time! Just say yes! Please!

"Well, I'd LOVE to see Lady Gaga in concert. And, I could use the break to get out of this town."

"Then we're on!"

"Ok! Thank you so much for thinking of me Tony!"

"Perfect! When you get into K.C. we can meet at one of my favorite restaurants. Bristol Seafood and Steak. It's right across from the center. You can Google and GPS it ok? Think you can get here by 5?

"That won't be a problem Tony! I'll see you then! And thank you! I'm excited!

"I am too. I'm looking forward to seeing you again Sonya.

"Sony! Please! Call me Sony!"

"Ok! Sony it is then. Talk later, ok Sony?"

"Yes! Sure! Please!"

"Ok! Bye!"

And so it was settled. Sonya didn't care if she *ever* got another job, or unemployment or hit the lottery. This was a glorious day! The day Tony Sanders called. She'd drive to Puerto Rico if that got her an evening with the illustrious Mr. Sanders.

CHAPTER 10

"Honey! I'm home!"

Bryan got home that evening around 7:30. Even on weekdays, he generally would go out for a few drinks with the boys. After ten years of marriage, his wife Sara had gotten used to it. They had two beautiful children, a boy 8 and a six-year-old girl. And, as Bryan wasn't around much, Sara did most of the parenting.

As usual, Bryan walked through the garage door into the kitchen. But what he saw was not what he'd expected.

There was Sara, crying breathlessly into what was already a soaked handkerchief.

"Baby! What's wrong! Are the kids ok?"

Still crying and gasping to catch air, she sobbed. "The kids are fine!"

"Well, what's wrong Babe? Are your folks ok?"

"I went to see my OB/GYN doctor today Bryan."

"Uh . . . Ok! What happened sweetie?"

"I've been having burning sensations when I urinate Bryan!"

Now, Bryan was concerned. That phone call from Sonya was real. He tried to act composed and confused about what she would say next, but he knew what was coming.

"Bryan, I have an STD! I have Gonorrhea!"

"What! Oh my God! Gonorrhea! How can that be?"

"He assured me I didn't get it from a toilet seat! He asked me if I had sex with anyone but my husband! It was so humiliating!"

Sara took her crying jag up a notch and now was near convulsing.

"Where have you been Bryan? What have you been doing? And who is Sonya?"

Bryan was big time busted. But still, he took an indignant stand.

"Sonya? What do you mean 'who is Sonya?' I don't know anyone named Sonya!"

"Well, her name and phone number was in your pant suit pocket Bryan! Was that some kind of magic trick? You're never home, you come in at all hours and now this! You've been cheating on me Bryan and now this! I'm so sick of it all!"

"Wait! Now I remember! Sonya was a real estate agent. I was looking around for a new house for us! I was gonna surprise you! Sonya was a real estate agent honey!"

"Really? Well then, you won't mind if I call her and ask her all about the new house you're looking at."

Bryan had to call her bluff and hope she wouldn't dial the phone.

"Sure! Please! Call her right now! Baby! I would never cheat on you."

Luckily, she demurred. The phone call would be more than she could handle in one day.

He was tempted to try to turn the tables on his wife and accuse her of having an affair; but thought better of it, lest he dig a deeper hole for himself.

"There's got to be a simple answer to this Sara. I don't have an STD. If I did, I'd have pain in my genitals too! Did your doctor give you a prescription?"

By now, Sara had calmed down some.

"Yes, he gave me some pills to take for 10 days. Said that should eliminate the infection."

"Well, that's good. Say, it's still early. Have you eaten yet?"

Sara hadn't eaten since the doctor visit. But she wasn't hungry.

"No, I'm going to bed Bryan. I've had a horrific day."

"Ok! I'll just make myself a sandwich. Don't worry, I'll get the kids in bed."

At this point the problem was far from resolved. But, at least things had calmed down a little. Sara's cry had morphed into the sniffles. Bryan would see his friend, Doctor Steve, tomorrow.

CHAPTER 11

"Busted"

As Friday morning came, Bryan attempted a conversation with Sara, but she wasn't in any mood to talk. She got the kids off to school and left Bryan alone in the house. She wouldn't be back anytime soon.

He finished a quick cup of coffee and called his friend doctor Steve. Could he get in today? Sure! If he could get in sometime in the next hour. That was no problem. Bryan was in his own hurry.

"Hey Bryan! What's up? Sinus Infection?"

"No! That's what I told your girl up front, I didn't want to tell her the real reason."

"Ok... what's the *real* reason?"

"Well, I came home last night to find my wife crying her eyes out. She went to her doctor and he told her she tested positive for Gonorrhea."

"Damn Bryan! That's serious trouble! You been sticking your pen in some strange ink?"

"That's the thing! Yeah! I've had some fun, but I don't have any symptoms of an STD."

"Well, that's pretty common, Bryan. Almost half the people who get an STD are asymptomatic. You could have it for years and not even know it. Let's get a urine and blood sample and see what comes up. Meanwhile, what are you gonna do about Sara? She must be beside herself. You sleep on the couch last night?"

"No, but she left early this morning without so much as a goodbye! Besides that, she found another woman's phone number in my suit pants when she took them to the dry cleaners. She's really on to me. I'm not sure what to do."

A few minutes later, the nurse came back with the results. Doctor Steve looked them over and:

"Well, congratulations Bryan, you're the proud owner of a good solid case of 'The Clap!', otherwise known as Gonorrhea."

"Damn!"

"The good news is, I can give you something that should nail it. I'm supposed to report it to the state, but I'll forgo that. The bad news is, sounds like you might be heading for divorce court."

"Yeah, I'm not sure what to do. You got any ideas?"

"Well, hopefully her doctor gave her a prescription. And, women don't really want to believe this kind of thing really happened. Just get this prescription filled and lay low for a while. Maybe if you ignore the subject, it'll just go away.

Bryan drove away from his doctor friend trying to figure out just where he might have picked this thing up.

"I'll bet that bitch Sonya gave it to me, then tried to blame it on me. Those other two women I had sex with were some time ago. I'm sure I got it from her."

* * *

About the time Bryan was leaving the doctor's office, Sonya received a call from a number she didn't recognize.

"Hello?"

"Hi! Is this Sonya?"

"Uh . . . yes. Who is this?"

"Sonya, my name is Sara Robbins. My husband is Bryan Robbins. Do you know him?"

Now, there was a long, pregnant pause in the conversation. Finally, Sonya spoke.

"Well, yes, sort of."

"What do you mean sort of? Are you doing some kind of real estate deal with him?"

"Look lady, I hardly know your husband and I don't deal in real estate. How did you get my number?"

"Well, did you have sex with my husband?"

The comment completely unnerved Sonya. She didn't know what to say or do. Finally, she yelled into the phone:

"I don't know your husband! Don't call me again!" and hung up.

That was enough for Sara Robbins. First, the woman said 'I *hardly* know your husband' then, she yelled that she *didn't* know her husband. And, of course, there was no real estate deal. Bryan Robbins just got caught with his hand in the cheating cookie jar.

With Bryan's lifestyle, coming home half drunk at all hours of the night, Sara has suspected for a long time that Bryan wasn't exactly the model husband. But, he was a good provider and with two kids running around the house, she had long ago decided to ignore her suspicions, as long as he didn't rub it in her face. But this, this was the nail in the coffin. It would be hard on the kids, but she would find a lawyer and file for divorce.

Meanwhile, across town in her apartment, Sonya was completely disquieted.

"Why didn't I just tell her I had sex with him but he didn't tell me he was married? Dammit! Please! Just leave me alone!"

She decided to save Mrs. Robbins phone number in her cell, just in case she called again. Next time, she could ignore the call. She would focus Tony Sanders and the Kansas City trip tomorrow. She hadn't been this excited in a long time.

Sonya tried to relax and put the phone call out of her mind, but the conversation just kept hanging around her thoughts.

"Maybe I shouldn't have hung up on her!"

Thankfully, Tony called that evening, just to confirm she'd be coming down for their rendevous. That took the edge off the worry.

"Hi Sony! It's Tony!

"Tony! It's so good to hear from you!"

"Great! I'm just calling to confirm you're coming down here tomorrow! I've got a great evening planned for you! Can you be here at the restaurant by 6?"

"Absolutely! I've been to K.C. many times. I'll leave here around two! That should get me right to the restaurant on time."

"Perfect! I'm excited to see you again Sony!"

"Me too Tony! See you soon!"

"Ok Babe! Bye now!"

"Babe! He called me BABE! He's excited to see me! That's what he said didn't he? He said, "I'm excited to see you!"

Sonya couldn't wait for tomorrow.

CHAPTER 12

"Oh, What a Night!"

Saturday morning. Sonya awakened with a serious case of what clinical psychologists call "Anticipatory Anxiety." It raises the blood pressure, kicks in the endorphins, and provides a glorious feeling of wellbeing.

In a couple of hours, she'd be making the drive to K.C. Camelot to have dinner and a concert, and maybe more, with Sir Lancelot Sanders.

"I'll leave around 2 O'clock, that should get me there in plenty of time I don't want to be too early. But what to wear? The last time he saw me, I didn't even have make up on! Not this time sister! I'll be dressed for success! High rise skinny jeans, and my Ivory, racer back tank top! No bra! My sexy red pumps would be perfect, but we're gonna do some walking. I'll wear my beige, lace up wedges. My hair's long enough, I can just drape it over my shoulder, show off the highlights. This watch is too cheap looking. I'll just put some bangles on my wrist," Full make-up this time: Foundation, Shadow, Mascara, "Come Hither" red lip color, some eyeliner, and my hunter green, crop leather jacket in case it gets cold in the auditorium. Besides, it picks up the green in my eyes.

Now, Mr. Sanders, meet the Sonya Hartiq I wanted you to see the first time we met!

Most of the morning, Sonya would be busy putting all of that together. She scolded herself for not having made a hair appointment, but it was too late by now. Anyway, she was pretty good at styling her hair on her own. She packed a satchel with extra lingerie, make up, blow dryer and a change of clothes for the trip home tomorrow, if it came to that.

No need to make a hotel reservation, on a weekend, she'd easily find a Holiday Inn Express or something around the area. Besides, Tony said he'd already made reservations for her at the Raphael in the Plaza. She'd seen it before when she visited K.C., but she'd never stayed there. Sonya looked it up on the net. Rooms started at $350 a night. She thought:

"What if he made the reservation but expects me to pay? OR, what if things don't go so well?"

Right on the money, at 2 p.m., Sonya jumped in the Toyota, flipped on the tunes and headed for Camelot. The drive between Omaha and Kansas City is literally all Interstate. Just head South and 3 hours later you're looking at the Kansas City International airport just to the right of I-29. Planes coming in for arrival fly very low right over the vehicles on the road below. The first time you experience it, it scares hell out of you because you don't see it coming and the sudden jet noise right on top of you is deafening. Look up, and there's a 737 so close, you feel you could reach up through the sunroof and touch it.

To Sonya's surprise, the time went by fairly quickly. The music on her Sirius XM radio, kept her attention and her mind from wandering too much into the future of the night.

With her I-phone GPS, she was able to zero right in on the restaurant and parking close by was surprisingly easy. Problem was, she was early. Tony said: "Dinner at 6" and it was only 5:45. She'd made good time on the trip, but if she got to the restaurant before he did, it just wouldn't feel right.

"He might be there already, but I don't want to take that chance. I'd rather be fashionably late than too early. I'd look too anxious. Well, I AM anxious, but I don't want him to see that."

And so, Sonya sat and waited in her car till 6 o'clock. She looked around for Tony's Subaru, but it wasn't to be found. There WAS a black BMW parked just up the street with a license plate that said "GANGSTA"

The Sprint Center was on one side of the street and the restaurant was on the other. Not much of a walk, either way. That was a comfort.

Just as soon as Sonya walked in the door, she spotted Tony talking with whom she presumed was the Maitre De' The man looked up at her and Tony turned around, big smile, walked over to her and hugged her.

"My God! He's even better looking than I remember! And that cologne!"

He could have walked right off the front cover of GQ Magazine. Tight jeans, crisp white dress shirt, unbuttoned at the collar, black alligator belt and dress shoes to match, and a gold Tissot watch secured by a black alligator band. Throw in the midnight black curly hair and blue eyes and he was a six foot something work of masculine wonderfulness.

"Sony! I'm so excited you're here! My God! Look at you! You're just gorgeous! Thank you for joining me tonight!"

The Maitre De came forward and interrupted the reunion:

"Mr. Messina, your table is ready sir, would you like to be seated?"

"Why yes, of course! Are you ready Sony?"

"Uh . . . yes, ok!"

"Perfect! Let's enjoy dinner"

He walked them over to a semi-secluded, private table at the back of the restaurant. Tony stood until the waiter pulled back Sony's chair so she could be seated.

Sonya was beside herself. She'd been to upscale restaurants before. She and her old boyfriend Robert went out occasionally, but this was like something right out of the movies. She felt like she was in a fog. The masculine scenery sitting across the table bordered on the unbelievable. She wanted to take her phone out and snap a picture of him, just to prove he was there with her, but she considered that that would be tacky and juvenile.

A moment later, their waiter appeared at the table out of nowhere.

"Good evening Mr. Messina!! It's good to see you again sir!"

Was she hearing things? She was sure they called him "Mr. Messina" twice now. *"Wasn't his last name Sanders?"*

"Good evening Robert! Before we order Could you please bring the wine list?"

"Robert! He DOES come here a lot!"

The waiter replied in a tone and dialect similar to the kind you'd expect from a Butler serving his wealthy benefactor.

"Most certainly sir!" And for the lady?"

"Sony would you like a glass of wine for starters?"

"Uh, yes! That would be fine!" Thank you!"

And once again:

"Excellent sir! I'll return momentarily!"

As promised, the waiter returned with the wine list and Tony perused it carefully.

"Well, Sony! What sort of wine would you prefer? I'm guessing maybe a refreshing white?"

"Yes, do you think they have a Moscato?"

"Hmm, I don't see it on here, but apparently you like a sweet white wine. They have a Riesling. Why don't I order a glass of it for you, I'm sure you'll love it, and if you don't, we'll just send it back!"

For all she cared, it could have been Kool Aid. She was just in a romantic trance. But what about this name thing?

"That will be fine Tony"

"There's a Charcuterie board on the menu, shall we share that for dinner? What do you think?"

CHARCUTERIE + CHEESE BOARD* prosciutto di parma, chorizo vela, seafood ceviche, romao rosemary cheese, burrata, poached pears, cornichons, red wine fig jam, baguette crostini 22

"Looks good to me! Let's do it!"

For much of life, the anticipation of something is so much more exciting than when it actually happens. But not this night. Just as Tony anticipated, Sonya loved the charcuterie. And the wine! She'd never had a Riesling before, but it brought sweet, magical things to her body.

"This wine is just incredible!"

And so, he ordered a second glass and then another. He had a second and third himself. They were becoming intoxicated, but the wine wasn't necessary for that condition. They were both intoxicated by their mutual chemistry before a drop of wine was poured. After some minutes of small talk, Tony rose from his chair, moved across the table, sat next to her and caressed Sonya's willing hand. It was happening. Those gloriously wild, untamed endorphins consuming your entire being with the almost unbearable pleasure of the realization that you and someone else have an intense, mutual attraction.

It's not love, but it's heading for the exits.

In those early, *"where have you been all my life?"* moments of a relationship, the other human just seems so perfect.

"Really! That's my favorite Ice cream too! I love Jazz! I wouldn't have guessed you like jazz!"

"Are you kidding me? You're not even allowed to live in K.C. if you don't like jazz! It's the law!"

"God! You look just radiant tonight!"

"Thank you, but I don't know what you see in me. A man like you must have a stable full of women calling you every day, begging for time with you"

"I know some women Sony, but not like you. To me, you're a woman in a world full of girls! Sweetie, would you like more wine?"

"Sweetie! He called me Sweetie!"

"Uh . . . yes! Sure! But first, can I ask you something?"

"Of course! And I'll be I know what it is. You want to know why everyone's calling me Mr. Messina, right?"

"Well, yes! I thought your name was Tony Sanders"

"Sony, Sanders is my professional name. I use it when I'm doing business out of town. I should have told you that the first time I met you. I apologize. My real name is Tony Messina, and just about everyone in this town knows me by that name. I hope you'll forgive me for introducing myself as Sanders. It's just that I had just met you and . . ."

"That's fine Tony. I feel better now that you've explained it. I was just sort of confused earlier when they called you Mr. Messina.

"Perfect! Now I can ply you with liquor!"

Sonya Thought:

"Ply away Mister!"

The restaurant was crowded, but for Tony and Sonya it was like being in a timeless bubble. They could see no one but each other. Soon, they were intertwining hands and just staring into each other's eyes. Minutes went by with no word spoken in either direction. The concert came and went. Neither of them noticed. There would be no Lady Gaga tonight. The consummate entertainment for the both of them was right at the corner table at the Bristol Steak and Seafood restaurant.

"I'm so sorry sir, but we're closing in 15 minutes. Is there something else I can bring you or the lady before we close?"

The spell was broken.

"What time is it? Damn! Uh no, we're fine Robert, just bring us the bill please! Sony! I'm so sorry, we missed the concert. I know you were really looking forward to it!"

"No Tony! It's fine! I've had a beautiful evening. Please don't worry. But it's late, I should drive home now."

"Absolutely not! I told you I've reserved a room for you at the Raphael! In fact, I'll drive you there! I'll have someone pick up your car in the morning."

Sonya was hoping Tony would say something like that, but protocol demanded she protest just a little.

"Oh! That's ok! Tony, I'll just find my way home, it's not a long drive"

"Not gonna happen. Sony. I insist. Do you have a change of close? Toothbrush?"

"Well, yes! They're in my car, just in case it got too late to drive home."

"Then let's get them. Give me your keys and I'll have a driver bring your car to the hotel in the morning"

"Well, alright, if it's not too much trouble"

Sonya would have happily just gone to Tony's house or apartment, whichever it was.

"Do you have a bag or suitcase?"

"Uh yes! I brought an overnight bag"

"Perfect! Just give me your keys and we'll take it to my car and get you set up for the night!"

And there it was, through her now blurred vision, Sonya saw the BMW with the "GANSTA" license plate she had seen earlier. It belonged to Mr. Tony Messina.

"Wow! What happened to the Subaru Outback? And why the vanity plate that said 'Gangsta'?

As one would expect, Tony opened the door for his newfound soul mate and after fifteen minutes of German Engineered driving, they pulled up to the front steps of the opulent Raphael Hotel.

"Good evening Mr. Messina! Shall we park your vehicle?"

"That won't be necessary Jason, I'm just checking my friend into her room. Please keep the car out front here, I'll be back in a bit"

"Very good sir!"

The Valet opened Sonya's door and Tony led her up the stairs. The effects of multiple glasses of wine made her lightheaded and she held onto Tony's arm all the way to the reception desk.

"Good evening Mr. Messina. How can we help you this evening?"

Sonya was taken aback by the greeting:
"Damn! Does EVERYBODY in this town know him?"

"Hello Katherine. I made a reservation this afternoon for Ms. Hartiq. We'd like to check in."

"Certainly sir! We have Ms. Hartiq's accommodations in the Premiere Suite as requested."

Sonya fumbled through her purse for her credit card, pulled it out and offered it to the desk clerk.

"Here you are Ma'am!"

"Your accommodations are taken care of Ms. Hartiq, I won't need your card. The Valet will bring your belongings up to your room shortly."

"Thank you, Katherine. If you'll give me the keys, I'll escort her, I know where the elevators are"

"Certainly sir! Here you are. I hope you enjoy your stay with us at the Raphael Ms. Hartiq"

Sonya was overwhelmed. Tony was going to escort her to her room.

"Did she say suite?"

"Well, here we are Sony! I can't tell you how much I enjoyed our evening together!"

Tony slid the electronic key into the lock and opened the door wide. Standing there, the gaze of longing captured both their eyes. He reached down and kissed her deeply. Sonya's arms willingly surrendered to his embrace.

"Now Tony! Now! I'm so ready! Stay with me! Make love to me!"

"Thank you so much for a beautiful evening Tony!"

"It was my pleasure babe. We'll get your car over to you in the morning. Sleep as long as you want. If you like I'll take you for breakfast downstairs, the restaurant serves an exquisite French Omelet"

"He's leaving? Oh, Tony please don't go!"

"Goodnight Sony! I can't wait to see you in the morning."

Just that fast, the caressing was over, and Tony Messina exited the room and worked his way down the hall to the elevators.

Sonya plopped herself down on the sofa in the suite living room.

"Oh my God! Just like that! And I was afraid he was a rapist or serial killer or something! Instead I get a gold medal, Olympic quality, GQ magazine gentleman! I <u>wish</u> he was a rapist!

Well, the night is over. But "Oh what a night!"

The Bellman brought up her night bag, and minutes later, Sonya removed her clothes, wiped her makeup and collapsed on the oversized bed, enveloping her in unworldly comfort. She began to pleasure herself, fantasizing Tony making love to her, but then, before she could finish, sleep overcame Sonya Hartiq.

CHAPTER 13

"How Suite It is!"

Sonya slept deep that night. Her final dream was about a collage of tiny bells ringing all at the same time.

"Wait! I'm not dreaming! That's the phone! The hotel room phone! Damn! Where is it? What time is it?"

"Hello?"

"Hi Sony! It's me Tony! Hope I didn't wake you!"

"Uh no! No! I was just getting into the shower.

"Great! Take your shower and come downstairs! I'll treat you to breakfast!"

Sony jumped in the shower. It was one of those walk-in types, lined with ceramic tile and no door; the kind one would see when you tour those mansion-like, parade of homes events. The rain soft shower head made her feel like she'd walked into a warm tropical downpour, minus the wind and thunder. If Tony weren't waiting downstairs, she would have just bathed in the liquid fantasy for hours.

She reluctantly walked out of the exquisite experience just moments later and hurried toward the suite vanity. No need to take out her blow dryer, or even her toothbrush. The Raphael provided such things. No time for heavy make up or eye liner and such. Just the basics. The extra black camisole with the cut-out sleeves she'd packed would come in handy, but she'd have to wear the same jeans as last night. And, no pumps. Her Nikes would have to do.

In Twenty-five-minutes flat, Sonya flew out the door to the elevators.

Fifteen seconds later the doors opened and presented her in all her morning glory to a smiling Tony. Coincidentally, she was dressed like her male counterpart, Nikes and all.

"Good morning Babe! Do you have a pact with the devil? No woman on this planet looks this good in the morning without divine intervention!"

"Babe! He called me Babe!"

"Flattery will get you everywhere mister!"

"Ok! Whaddya say! Let's eat!"

The Restaurant on the ground floor of the Raphael was called "Chaz on the Plaza" To label it "upscale" would be an understatement. The Sunday Brunch was all a "Morning After Cinderella" could ask for. Chaz Lobster Bisque Soup and Apple Manchego Salad with Red & Green Apples, Shaved Manchego Cheese with a Lemon Shallot Vinaigrette, topped off with Coconut Pineapple Mimosas and romantic conversation.

"Sony! I hope you're enjoying this!"

"You're spoiling me Tony. This whole weekend has been wonderful! And so are you! I hate having to leave!"

"Then don't!"

"Then don't? What do you mean?"

"I mean, you can stay another night here! The hotel manager owes me one, and the tab is covered! Or, you can stay at my place tonight if you prefer! Call in sick for work tomorrow! You like Jazz? There's some good Jazz seven nights a week at the Green Lady Lounge up on Grand Boulevard, and OJT is playing there tonight. They're my favorite group. We can make a night of it again and you can leave in the morning."

"Call in sick tomorrow. That's a good one! If only I had a job to call!"

"You mean it Tony? You would let me stay at your place?"

"I hope you will! I promise to be a gentleman!"

"Don't be a gentleman on my account mister!"

"Well ... "

"Great! Then it's settled! Let's finish our mimosas and get your things."

"What about my car Tony? Should I just follow you to your place?"

"You can hop in my car! I'll have the Hotel valet drive it over, they know where I live, it's just up the street and I have a private parking space for you."

Sonya was having a hard time believing this was really happening. Everything seemed so surreal! Romance and high adventure! Right out of a fairy tale book. Only thing missing was the glass slipper, and she figured he probably had that waiting for her in his house. Apartment? She'd soon find out.

CHAPTER 14

"Dance with me!"

As it turned out, Tony lived in an apartment just a few minutes away from the Plaza. It was housed in a 25-story apartment complex called One Light, adjacent to the Kansas City Power and Light District, basically, the pulse of the city. It was immediately apparent to Sonya, that this was where the city's beautiful people congregated.

As they pulled into the private, underground parking garage, Sonya noticed that someone had already parked her Toyota right next to where Tony pulled in. in her bewilderment, Sonya could just sit and stare at her vehicle. Then Tony, quickly got out of the Gangsta mobile, walked around to the passenger side and opened the door for his love interest.

"Welcome to my humble abode Madam! I hope it will meet your expectations!"

Sonya was speechless. Once he had held out his hand and helped her out of the car, he closed the passenger door and walked the two steps to her Toyota. Just as he had instructed, the driver, Sonya's keys were sitting on top of the left front tire hidden by the front fender.

"Here's your keys Babe! Let me get your overnight bag and we'll head up to the apartment"

The apartment was, in a word, astonishing. Sonya was instantaneously taken aback, not just by the luxuriousness, but also the pristine surroundings. Not a speck of dust anywhere; a place for everything and everything in its place. The entire apartment was enveloped by floor to ceiling windows, affording a three hundred sixty-degree view of the city twenty-three floors below.

"Tony! This place is magnificent!"

"Thank you, Sony, I like living here, it's got everything I need. There's even a grocery store attached to the building downstairs. Roof Top pool and bar, wine room, fitness center, the works!"

Sonya wondered what a place like this must cost. She'd never seen an apartment like this before. The kitchen even had an island for food preparation. It was certainly a far cry from her apartment in Omaha.

"Here! Let me get your bag! I have a guest bedroom for you just over there."

"Seriously? I hope you're just being polite Tony, because that guest bedroom is not my preferred destination."

"There you go Sony! Let's sit down and relax for a bit. We just had breakfast, but I've got some wine and meats and cheeses in the fridge. I've got a bottle of Moscato. Will that work for you?"

"That's perfect! Thank you, Tony!"

Just then, Tony's cell phone rang.

"Damn! I sorry Babe, this is a business call. I have to take it. Can you excuse me for a bit?"

"Sure! That's fine!"

With that, Tony walked away and into the master bedroom closing the door. Sony could hear "some" of the conversation from in the living room, but most of it was muffled.

"Well, how late is this guy? I can't do anything tonight, I have company. I'll pay him a visit tomorrow and get his money. Chicago? Who the hell's in Chicago? What's the ticket? Five- grand? I'm not going to Chicago for five-grand! The price is ten plus expenses. That's my price! Ten-grand plus or let someone else handle it. Meanwhile, I'll pay a visit to Mr. Gabardino tomorrow. Talk later."

While she couldn't hear much of the conversation, Sonya had never heard that tone of voice from Tony before. He was very assertive, sounded almost angry. He emerged from the bedroom with a kind of flush on his cheeks.

"Sorry about that Babe! Business stuff! So… let me get that wine and cheese now."

"So Tony, you said you're a contractor?"

"Yep! I've been contracting for almost 10 years."

"Business must be good huh?"

"It's a living. But sometimes I work long hours. It takes me all over the country. I might have to go to Chicago next week. I should apologize. Speaking of that, how's your job going?

"Well, I didn't tell you about this, but I resigned my position last week."

Sonya didn't want to tell him she'd been fired.

"Oh! Well then, that's good news! You won't have to call in sick to work tomorrow!"

"No, but I have to get back to Omaha Tony, I've got some loose ends to tie up."

As the day rolled on, the conversation went down that familiar road that we all experience when we first begin to fall in love.

"What's your favorite ice cream?"

"Butter Pecan"

"Wow! Mine too! You like lasagna? I make a mean lasagna!"

"I *love* lasagna! Maybe I can coerce you to make it for me sometime!"

Wine and cheese and hours of *"You too? That's incredible!"* conversation led up to the time to go out for some Sunday evening Jazz at the Green Lady Lounge. Sunday night parking was easy, right across from the street of the bar/lounge. As you walked in, it was like entering a retroactive time machine. Right out of the 1950's or even the 40's! Walls painted scarlet red, covered with gold framed, vintage oils painted by obscure artists a hundred years ago. Midcentury lights adorned the marble bar. It was intimacy personified. Looked like one of those smoky bars you'd see in some old black and white movie, minus the smoke. Sonya loved jazz, but she'd never heard it performed so well. Jazz groups in Omaha tried, but it wasn't the same. Tony said the band was his favorite, but she surmised that any group who played this venue was top drawer.

It was busy, even for a Sunday night, but they were seated just a few feet from the band, immediately holding hands at the table. Tony ordered for her a drink called the "Prickly Pear" and a Black Walnut Manhattan for himself. Sonya fell into an almost meditative state. The music was mesmerizing and holding hands with Tony sent electric emotions through her entire being. It was as close to heaven as she'd ever been.

The music stops at 7:30 p.m. on Sundays. Time to leave.

"Sweetie, would you like to go out for dinner?"

"I don't think so Tony. I'm not really that hungry. Can't we just pick something up on the way home?"

"Sure! In fact, like I said, there's a grocery store attached to the apartment building. They're open Sunday's till nine. Let's do that!"

Home by 8:20 p.m. they walked in the grocery store, picked out some baguette bread, black forest ham, a head of lettuce, provolone cheese, some strawberries and whipped cream (just in case,) and headed upstairs. Tony cut up the baguette and put together the perfect late evening snacks.

"Want some more wine Sony?"

"No thanks honey *(did I call him honey?)* I'm about wined out."

"It's too bright in here, don't you think?"

Not bothering to answer, he dimmed the lights.

He brought the strawberries, whipped cream and some vanilla flavored seltzer water over to the coffee table next to the sofa. The sandwiches would have to come later.

"There we go! These strawberries look good!"

With that, he picked one up, dipped it in the cream and brought it to her eager, waiting lips.

"Now we're getting somewhere Mr. gentleman Messina!"

Sonya reciprocated and Tony hungrily obliged her offering. This went on for several minutes until on the next strawberry adventure, Tony leaned over with one of the delicious morsels placed strategically in his lips and placed it onto hers, sharing a strawberry kiss that immediately turned passionate. Sonya willingly laid back onto the sofa as Tony softly laid his body on top of her. Arms entangled, her legs wrapped around his torso, this is what she came for.

The embrace was intense. The kisses unimaginably lascivious. He gently caressed her breast and then . . .

"Let's go in the bedroom!"

Sonya didn't answer. She didn't have to. He knew she was ready. He got up off the sofa grabbed her hand, shutting off the living room lights, and led her to his bed.

As are most women, Sonya was insecure about her body. He had never seen her unclothed before. Would he be disappointed? Repulsed? Too late for those musings, mutual passion had taken over the moment

Tony moved first, gently pulling her camisole over her head, revealing her braless nipples, which, if truth be told, he had been admiring secretly whenever he thought she wasn't looking.

He wanted her from the very first day in that coffee shop weeks ago. And now it was happening.

Sonya could tell that the way he looked at her, he was more than pleased with what her body had to offer. He was already hard. And so, encouraged by his body's involuntary reaction, she unbuckled his belt.

As she pulled it aside and drew down the barrier that were his jeans, she took his coveted manhood into her lips and stroked it with her moistened tongue; forgetting now, in her nakedness, that he might take notice of her imperfect body. Her too small breasts and those stubborn extra pounds, methodically applied and placed by Mother Nature's cruel joke in places not easily hidden from a discerning lover.

But Tony was paying no mind to Sonya's perceived bodily imperfections. His penis swelled evermore intense. Harder. His entire universe was focused on one place, one person. He could think of nothing else but the unimaginable pleasure now pulsating in his groin.

But he didn't want to climax this way. Not tonight, not now. He gently reached down to her and whispered for her to stop.

"He doesn't like it?"

He softly pulled her up to him and tenderly holding her head in his hands, he brought her to himself in fiery passionate kisses, provoking the most intense seduction.

It was fantasy made real.

And now, the dance began. Slowly, gently, he introduced his hardness to her, now wet with desire.

As he guided himself inside her, Sonya gasped with indescribable pleasure. This man, this Prince, was taking her to emotional, erotic islands, she hadn't been before. The heat between them had spawned incandescence. Her nipples erupted swaying back and forth across his hardened chest. His penis brought only loving pleasure. They moved together in perfect rhythm, her rising up to him and him with gentle thrusts moving deep inside her.

Alternately kissing her and drawing loving circles with his tongue on her erect nipples. she responded with moans of womanly pleasure.

What went on for almost an hour, seemed like mere moments; then, they came together in unison.

They kissed each other tenderly, rolled over, and both exhausted by the violent ecstasy, sweet sleep came over them.

CHAPTER 15

"He's so fine!"

Both Tony and Sonya slept in a satisfied bliss. Several times, he rolled over in a twilight daze and put his arm around her. She instinctively pressed her body up into him, still unconsciously satisfied.

Tony awakened before Sonya, quietly got up out of their bed of harbored lust and quietly walked himself into the kitchen. Breakfast would be ready and waiting for his newfound love when she woke from her sleep. Bacon, eggs, hash browns, wheat toast and even orange juice and coffee were on the unsolicited menu. Among his myriad talents, Mr. Messina could also cook.

The welcoming sounds and scents of sizzling bacon and eggs and coffee aromatically woke Sonya. She stumbled out of the bedroom, his body's scent still lingering on her skin and the residue of sleep not yet quite out of her system, she dropped herself down on the living room couch. Hearing her entrance, Tony turned from the stove with a cheery "Good morning babe! Breakfast is almost ready. I hope you like your eggs scrambled!"

She did.

He brought the entire ensemble over to the coffee table next to the sofa and they enjoyed breakfast together, each still glowing from the surreal night before. But now it was Monday. Back to reality. Sonya would have to reluctantly drive the three and a half hours back to Omaha and Tony would be making a collection stop at a strip club on the other side of the city.

Neither spoke much while they consumed the morning's nourishment. Mostly loving smiles and light caresses. They had said and done it all the night before.

Secretly to herself, Sonya wondered:

"Is this going to be it? Are we finished? Will I ever see him again?"

And, just as the thought crossed her mind, Tony revealed his intentions.

"Say Babe, as I told you, I might have to go to Chicago next week. Would you like to meet me there for the weekend?"

"Oh Tony! I'd love to, but I just can't afford it right now. I'm job hunting and I don't even get unemployment."

"Well, if that's all that's stopping you, please don't worry, you can't job hunt on the weekend! I'll get your plane ticket and pick you up at Midway in the rental car. On the other hand, I don't want to pressure you and assume you'd like another weekend with me."

"No! No Tony! It sounds fantastic. The whole weekend has been like a fairy tale for me. I've fallen for you Tony. I just don't want to sponge off you. You've been so generous!"

"Well, guess what Babe! I'm falling too. And if all it takes to see you again is the price of a plane ticket from Omaha to Chicago, I'd pay that a thousand times. Just say you'll go, and I'll take care of the rest."

"Well, when you put it like that, then yes! I'm in Mr. Messina!"

"Perfect! Then it's settled. I'll get back to you about it once I know I have to go"

"Look at the time! It's almost 10 a.m.! I better get ready to leave!"

"Yeah, I have work to do today too Babe. If you want to clean up, just use the shower off my bedroom."

It wasn't something she would ordinarily do before a long drive, but after Sonya showered, she carefully applied full facial make up in preparation for her exit. She wanted him to remember how she looked in the best way possible.

She gathered her things in her bag, walked out and announced:

"Well sweetie! I'm ready!"

As they now had revealed their feelings for one another, they were now both freely in the "Sweetie," "Babe," "Honey," stage of the relationship. It was satisfying. Tony escorted her down to her Toyota, opened the back door, placed her bag in the back seat, then opened her door, waited for her to get in place in the driver's seat, then leaned over and the deepest, most passionate goodbye kiss went on between them for an almost entire Kansas City minute.

Tony stood and waved and watched Sonya disappear into the morning traffic. Then went up to the

Apartment to put himself together for the day ahead.

Driving back home, Sonya could hardly believe the weekend happened. She knew it was real, but it didn't seem real. It was dreamlike. The best dream of her entire life. Problems were waiting for her back in Omaha, but they didn't loom as large as when she left for K.C. last Saturday morning. Her aura shed romance sparklers inside the Toyota all along I-29 North heading home.

It was Monday alright, and Monday was turning out to be her favorite day of the week. Life was good! Job or no job!

About an hour up the road just approaching Saint Joe, Missouri, the phone rang. She kept it close to her and on vibration, just in case Tony decided to call her on her trip back. She glanced down at the number but didn't recognize it. It wasn't Tony but, it was an Omaha number. She picked up.

"Hello?"

"Is this Sonya?"

She didn't recognize the voice at first. Then . . .

"Bryan Robbins! Why are you calling me?"

"Listen you fucking bitch! You gave me the 'clap' and I'm just calling to let you know you're gonna pay! You better sleep with one eye open you dirty, little cunt!"

Rattled by his words, Sonya hung up spontaneously.

"Oh my God! He used the "C" word! What am I going to do? How did I get caught up in this thing? Maybe I should call the police! Oh my God!"

The phone rang again. Same number.

This time, she didn't answer. Her hands were shaking on the steering wheel.

"What was he going to do to her?"

Now she was really scared.

"Oh Tony! Please call me! I need to talk to you!"

Back in Omaha again, it was time for Sonya's "reality sandwich." She had only been gone since Friday and her mailbox was already stuffed; mostly with overdue bill notices. As she opened them one after another, they all basically said the same thing:

"Friendly Reminder!"

Did you forget to make a payment? We appreciate your business and understand that sometimes life events can make us forgetful.

If you've already made payment, we thank you and apologize for this reminder.

In the event you haven't yet made your payment, please do so at your earliest opportunity and thank you again!

Sincerely,

Blah Blah Blah

Sonya thought: *"No need to apologize folks! I have no money to pay my bill!"*

CHAPTER 16

"Mob Money"

T ony would call her later to make sure she arrived home safely. He was smitten just like her. She wasn't his first love, but she could wind up being his last. He'd dated some sizzling hot ladies but there was something special about Sony.

"I can't wait to see her this weekend."

But Tony had a job to do today. Back up in the apartment, he grabbed his "Louisville Slugger" baseball bat and, for good measure the 9mm Glock automatic he kept in his dresser drawer under his underwear and socks. Too big for his pockets, Tony stuck the gun behind his jacket between his shirt and belt.

Joseph "Fat Joey" Gabardino was almost a month late with the vig at his strip club, and it was Tony's job to play collection agency.

The strip joint was just across the road from Arrowhead Stadium. Lots of guys would float over there to watch and play with the ladies after the games. Pole dancing, lap dances, and private rooms where the boys could go a little further if they had the price.

He pulled up to the club about 1 p.m., grabbed his bat and walked with confident bad intentions up to the front door. Inside, he was immediately confronted by the daytime bouncer Sammy Cosentino. Sammy was the stereotypical door guard gorilla. Big head, small brain, large muscles and the perfunctory scar on his cheek from a previous encounter with a knife wielding drunk.

Bad Ass that he was, Sammy wouldn't mess with Tony. He knew Tony, and he knew why he was there and, more importantly, who sent him. You mess with Tony Messina and you're messing with the K.C. mob.

On March 20, 2009, "Blackhand Strawman", a documentary of Kansas City's organized crime history was released in theaters in Kansas City. The Kansas City mob wasn't what it used to be in the 70's, 80's and 90's when Tony's dad was working things. In fact, by the 2000's there were less than 12 made men in the whole organization but, Tony Messina was one of them. Despite its diminished influence, the K.C. mob still ran things in the Metropolitan area and the entire states of Missouri, Nebraska, Oklahoma, Las Vegas and Washington DC. Jules Infantino still ran things with an iron fist. Extortion, prostitution, drugs, loan sharking, the whole gamut.

"Hey Sammy!"

"Hey Tony! What's up?"

"Joey here?"

"uh"

"Not 'uh' Sammy! Where is he? In the back?"

"Yeeeah!"

Without another word, Tony walked right past Sammy and into the club. It was a seedy looking place, as one might expect. A near nude dancer wearing open toed clear acrylic heels was swinging around a steel pole on one leg, bent at the knee.

It wasn't really busy this early in the day, only about a half dozen men, gawking at the dancing nude or sitting with one of the other scantily clad ladies buying her drinks at fifteen bucks a pop.

Mr. Gabardino's office was in the back, with a sign on the door that read: "Private Employees Only"

Tony knew where to go; he had been here before. As he approached the office, he expected it to be locked, but it wasn't. With a firm hand he twisted the knob and walked in, bat in hand. He literally caught Joseph "Fat Joey" Gabardino with his pants down, sitting in a chair with a woman's head bouncing up and down between his legs.

When Tony entered, Gabardino jumped up knocking the young woman over backwards. And now, standing there, his pants fell to the floor revealing his middle aged, belly flapped paunch. He didn't get the nick name "Fat Joey" by missing many meals.

"Tony! Hey! It's good to see you!"

"I'm sure it is! So good, I bet you want to give me some cash!"

Just then, the young woman had pulled herself up, grabbed the edge of the desk with both hands and peeked over the top to gaze upon a Greek God standing in the middle of the room with a baseball bat waving back and forth in his hand.

Pointing at her with the bat, almost in a whisper, Tony calmly ordered her out of the room.

"You can go now!"

With that, the young woman stood up, walked around the desk, and giving Tony a wide berth, passed him gingerly on the way to her exit.

"You're late Joey!"

"No! No! Tony! What do you mean?"

"I mean you're late, and I don't have time for your B.S. Do I have to use this thing? Eight large NOW Joey or this place gets busted up and you with it!"

"Tony! I don't have eight Grand! Give me a couple days, and I'll get it for you."

"Joey! I'm not gonna tell you again. Pull your pants up, go to your safe and get me the juice!"

"Ok! Ok! But I don't have the whole thing Tony!"

"How much you got?"

"I'll open the safe and show you! Honest Tony! "I don't have that much!"

Joseph "Fat Boy" Gabardino's hands trembled as he slid over a small cabinet. Underneath, the safe appeared, cemented into the floor. After two futile tries, he managed to turn the proper combination and pull open the door. Tony stood over him the entire time, just in case Mr. Gabardino had a piece in the safe and some foolish idea.

As it turned out, there was a Smith & Wesson Chief's Special on one of the shelves, but Joey was frozen with fear. He wasn't going to reach for it in any event.

"Grab the cash Joey! All of it!"

The fat man pulled out several bundles of cash wrapped in yellow paper bands that had $1000 printed on them.

"Here you are Tony! See! It's all I have! Six Thousand Dollars!"

"That's not enough! Get me the other two Grand."

"Tony! You can see! I don't have it!"

"Then go out front and get it out of the cash register"

"I can't do that! It's my working cash!"

"Then I'll do it for you. ."

He knew not to push this thing any further. He walked out to the front with Tony following. He pushed his front desk clerk aside and opened the register. The top drawer was full of twenties, tens' and fives' and underneath were the hundreds; the entire take from last night's entertainment and the afternoon's cover charges.

"Here you are! $1347! That's it Tony! That's the whole enchilada! Please! Give me a break! I'll get the rest. Tomorrow."

"How much is in your pocket?"

"My pocket? You want what's in my pocket?"

"Listen Joey! You're $653 short! That's just about the cost of a broken knee cap. I don't have time for this! Empty your pockets!"

Reaching into his pocket, Gabardino pulled out a wad of hundreds.

"Hand it over! One, two, three, four, five, six, seven, eight! Ok! I'll keep the extra change for old times' sake. Don't be late again Joey! The old man's losing his sense of humor about you!"

Without another word, Mr. Messina exited with eight thousand, one hundred forty- seven dollars and drove away, a hard day's work now completed. He was glad he didn't have to break any bones. He really disliked that part of the job. He'd do it if he had to, but he had no taste for it.

Tony immediately drove over to deliver the "Vig" to Mr infantino.

Julian Infantino would come in most days around 11 a.m. to play cards with his cronies, have a burger, hold the cheese, and wash it down with a cheap chianti. To the unknowing eye, Jules "The Machete" Infantino was just a simple old man going through his daily routine. He sometimes wore the same disheveled clothes for days in a row. To come across him on the street, one might be tempted to throw him a couple of bucks for a sandwich; but in Kansas City, all the mob money came to him and through him.

Tony pulled up outside "Uncle Jimmy's," parked his car next to an expired meter and hopped into the bar. Tony walked to the back table where he knew Julian would be holding court. There he sat with three rough looking thugs, a deck of cards and a glass of wine.

"I've got Fat Joey's money for you sir!"

"Tony! Good to see you son! So, you have something for the old man?"

"Yes sir! Eight Large!"

"Nice! Very Nice!"

Tony handed him a thick white envelope and Julian just sat it down on the table in front of him, not bothering to count the bills inside. He knew no one, least of all Tony Messina, was going to short him his due.

After some small talk, Julian opened the envelope and counted out eight hundred.

"Here you go son! Here's your end! Ten percent

"It's ok Mr. Infantino, five hundred will do it. I nudged Fat Joey for some extra!

Julian Infantino turned to the guys on the other side of the table.

"You see that! That's why I like this kid! He's a hundred percent! None of youse guys would have told me if you strong armed a little extra! You take all eight Benji's Tony! Don't worry about it! Nice work!"

"Uh ... Mister Infantino there is something I'd like to talk to you about."

"Ok. What's on your mind Tony?"

"Well, Freddy Cosenta called me about a Chicago gig"

"I'm aware! What about it?"

"Well, they're paying just Five grand for the whole shebang."

"Five Grand! For Chicago?"

"That's what I thought! By the time I pay for a plane ticket, room and car rental, I'll have five large in expenses. I'd like the job, but it's worth at least ten grand plus."

"I see what you mean son! Not to mention the risks. You want the contract? I'll call Freddy. They've got the juice. He's probably skimming off the top. Freddy's tight that way. Nobody else is gonna do it for five large. Don't worry about it, I'll talk some sense into him and get back to you later today ok?"

"Yes, sir! Thanks so much!"

It was an entirely different Tony who stood in front of Jules Infantino compared to the strong-arm gangster he portrayed at the strip club. This was the courteous, polite, well mannered, young Tony Messina. He left the bar knowing Jules would fix it for him. Now, he'd call Sony and tell her to pack for a weekend in Chicago.

"Hello Tony?"

"Hi Babe! What's up?"

"I'm so glad you called! I've had a terrible morning!"

"What's wrong sweetie? What happened?"

"I can't talk about it right now Tony, it's just good to hear your voice."

Sonya didn't want to let Tony in on the phone call from Bryan Robbins. How could she explain it all?

Tell him she'd had an STD and the guy who gave it to her was threatening her? She'd just keep it all to herself.

"Well, ok! I have some good news! I got the Chicago contract; we're going to Chicago this weekend!"

"Oh Babe, I'm not sure I should go."

"Why? You don't like me anymore?"

"Don't be silly. It's just that I'm job hunting and... "

"Sony! Like I said! It's the weekend! You can't job hunt on the weekend! Anyway, I already bought your ticket. I'm on a different flight but we both land at Midway five minutes apart! I'm in Friday at 1:20 and yours lands at !:25. I'll be waiting at the gate. Can't wait to see you!"

"Well, how do I get the ticket?"

"I'll e-mail it to you. It's Southwest. Just bring it down to the airport. You really don't even have to do that, but you'll probably feel better that way. You're in the system. You just need to show up."

"Ok babe. I'm excited to see you!"

"Me too! We'll have fun! You hang in there. You'll find a job soon. And if you don't, we'll take more trips!

Love you!"

"Alright honey. Love you too! Please call me later!"

"Ok... I've gotta go. Talk later."

"He said he loved me! Loved me! And HE said it first! That fixes my day! To hell with Bryan Robbins!

CHAPTER 17

"Guess who's coming to dinner!"

Tuesday. As usual, Bryan got home late that night. Even on weekdays he somehow seemed to have to work late; meeting with some client for an "after work" cocktail.

He was three sheets to the wind when he finally pulled into the garage, 7:30 p.m.

As was his custom, Bryan stumbled into the kitchen through the attached garage door. There was Sara sitting down at the kitchen table. A well-groomed, middle aged man sat next to her in a business suit. Striped tie, Immaculate white starched shirt, and if Bryan could see them, super shined, wing tipped, Florsheim shoes.

Bryan was taken aback by the scene. Both his wife and the man had a scowl on their faces.

"Hi babe! Where's the kids? Who's this?"

"Bryan, this is my divorce attorney Karl Steier"

"Nice to meet you! Seriously Babe, where're the kids?"

"Seriously Bryan. Say hello to Mr. Steier"

"Hello Mr. Steier! Now, what's this all about?"

"I'm divorcing you Bryan!"

"C'mon!"

Looking over at the attorney in an almost drunken stupor Bryan says:

"Seriously! You selling insurance? Cause you look like an insurance man! Sara! Where's the kids?"

"No sir! I'm a divorce attorney. Your **wife**'s divorce attorney."

"Honey! Tell him to quit screwing around. It's not funny Mr. Stabler, or whoever you are.

Sara looked at him solemnly "You're right Bryan. It's not funny and it's Mr. Steier. Guess who I talked to?

"Darth Vader! How the hell should I know?"

Does the name Sonya Hartiq ring a bell?

"Who?"

"Sarah Hartiq?

"Uh"

"You know! The real estate woman you gave VD."

"I don't know what you're talking about."

"Oh yes you do Bryan, I called that woman whose number was in your dry cleaning, and you probably know a hundred more just like her! She told me all about how you met her at the Interlude and spent the night at her apartment."

Even in his drunken state, Bryan was ready to commit emotional suicide. This guy really *was* a divorce attorney.

"I don't know what that woman told you but, like I said, she was a realtor."

"Sure, you do Bryan. She's our realtor, Sonya! Did you know that she hadn't had sex in almost two years before you? And then you gave her *and me* an STD!"

At this point, the lawyer felt compelled to join in and earn his retainer. He bent over the table and handed a folded piece of legal paper to Bryan Robbins and exclaimed: "Mr. Robbins, consider yourself served."

"Served what?"

"Divorce papers Mr. Robbins."

"Oh c'mon! Baby you can't do this! We have children! You! Mr. Steikler! Or whatever the hell your name is, you get the hell out of my house."

"Mr. Robbins, I'm afraid you're the one who's going to have to leave. Your wife doesn't want you in this house anymore"

Bryan looked over at his wife. The look on her face wasn't sad or hurt. It was simply furious. Hell, hath no wrath . . .

"Baby! Is this really what you want?"

"Just go away Bryan. I'll see you in court. Bring your girlfriends if you like!"

"Well, where do I go? I don't know where to go!"

"That, my dear, falls under the category of 'Not my problem'

Once again, the attorney worked to earn his pay. "Mr. Robbins, you have to leave now sir."

Bryan was dumbstruck. "Ok! I'm leaving! But I'll get my own attorney! Then we'll see!"

"I would advise you to do that sir. You're going to need one."

With that, Bryan turned toward the garage door and halfway out the door yelled back: "Sara! Please call me later!"

Sara didn't answer. She just watched him go. She'd taken the kids to her mom's right after school. Except for her and the attorney, the house was empty.

"Would you like to have a drink Karl?"

"uh Sure!"

"Good! And afterwards, I'll give you a tour of the house!"

The surprise confrontation with Sarah and her attorney took all the wind out of Bryan's sails.

He could hardly believe it. In all the years they'd been together, he'd never seen her like this.

"That attorney poisoned her! I bet they're high fiving right now! This is all so wrong! I didn't even get my toothbrush before I left. Well, I better find a place to stay tonight. I don't want to go to Stan's couch. Maybe I'll get a hotel room, call her in the morning. She'll be more reasonable once she has a chance to sleep on it."

Actually, Sara and her attorney were doing much more than 'high fiving.' *"Hell, hath no wrath like a woman scorned."*

The next morning:

"Hello!"

"Sarah! It's me!"

"I know who it is. What do you want Bryan?"

"Honey, I spent the night at the Holiday Inn Express!"

"Good for you! I hear they have a terrific breakfast!"

"So, you're still mad at me?"

"I'm not mad at you Bryan, I'm divorcing you!"

"C'mon sweetie, you can't do that! After all these years?"

"I'm doing it Bryan. Count on that!"

"Babe! We have children! What about the kids?

"And you have girlfriends!" What about your girlfriends?"

"Aww, c'mon! I don't have any girlfriends! I love you!"

"Whatever Bryan. Just go away. The kids will be fine. You can visit on weekends."

"So, you want me to get an attorney?"

"I want you to do whatever you feel is best for you. You're a serial cheater Bryan. I'm sure you've been cheating on me for years. Maybe even from the start of our relationship."

"That's just not true Sarah!"

"Well, just what IS true Bryan? Is it true that you gave me an STD?"

"I can explain that!"

"No. You can't Bryan. Or, at least not to me. You can explain it to the judge in divorce court."

"Your bags are packed and sitting in the garage. I've changed all the locks, and when you come by for your things, leave your garage door opener on the steps inside."

"Oh Baby! C'mon!"

"Save your 'Oh Babies' for your girlfriends Bryan."

"Alright! Alright! I'll be over later to pick things up"

"That's fine! Don't bother to knock. I won't be here, and the house will be locked up."

"I see."

"I'm glad you do. Have a great day. Bye"

Sarah hung up, leaving the ominous dial tone flaring in Bryan's ear. He'd crossed the line with her this time. It scared and flustered him. If she went through with this, and it looked like she was going to, life as he knew it was over.

CHAPTER 18

"Preparations"

F riday couldn't come fast enough for either of them. That euphoria that overtakes you when you first realize you're falling in love. With all the relationships and beautiful women, the 37-year- old Tony Messina had experienced, none of them took hold of him like Sonya Hartiq.

For her part, Sonya, for the first time in her life, finally knew what love felt like. Her first serious relationship was with Robert, but it never, ever felt like love. It obviously did for Robert, he bought a ring and did the whole bended knee thing, though somehow, it never felt right for her.

But this, this was different. Gloriously different! Tony Messina was at the top of her thoughts all day, every day.

She occupied a good part of his day as well, but something else kept creeping into his consciousness. This new relationship was nudging him into examining just who he was. He was becoming worried about his mental state. Was he Bi-polar? One minute he could be the most polite and congenial individual, the next his short-fused temper would flare for some small, insignificant slight and he'd be ready to kill you.

"In fact, that was *this* job wasn't it?"

There was no bad temper involved here, it was all about money.

"But maybe that's worse!" He thought.

They say that the more frequently you do something, commit some sin, the easier it gets the second or third or twenty-third time. Through experience, Tony Messina knew that to be true. He had put an end to many lives, and these days it was just a job. No emotional attachment or regret was involved.

Why did he invite her to come along? He knew better than to mix business with pleasure. He just wanted more of her. More time. More of everything about her.

He had already made cash purchases of 3 different "burner" cell phones from an obscure gas station convenience store just off Interstate 29. With one of these, Tony could talk to his Chicago contacts anonymously. When he was finished talking, he'd just throw the phone away. The individual on the other end also had a burner, so nobody, Feds or otherwise, could trace the calls made to these anonymous, disposable random numbers.

His luggage included a Soviet made PSS silent pistol, also called the MSS "VUL". Created in 1980 for assassinations. The perfect weapon for such assignments. Just 6 inches in length, and completely silent when fired; eliminating noise, smoke, blast or flash from the barrel. It sounds like a child's clicker gun. Used by Russian Special Forces, it is rare for anyone in the West to possess this enigmatic ordnance, but Mr. Messina had one of the few.

Not being sure if he would have the opportunity to even use the handgun in the commission of his contract, he also packed a syringe loaded with a high dose of a fentanyl drug derivative, Carfentanil. One hundred times more potent than fentanyl which, itself, is 100 times more potent than Heroin. Both drugs work to depress respiration, which can quickly lead to coma and death. But, while there is an antidote for a fentanyl overdose, if administered within 30 minutes, there is no time for an antidote for the intensely more powerful Carfentanil. Tony would have to be careful. Even touching a miniscule amount of this opioid on your finger, could end your own life within minutes. He packed the syringe gingerly in cloth and bubble wrap.

Once again, just as he did with the rental company for the trip to Omaha, Tony used the surname Sanders for his flight reservations. He still had all the documentation he'd need. Driver's license, credit cards, even a passport with his picture and the name Anthony Sanders imbedded right alongside it.

Meanwhile, Sonya went fashion shopping with the one credit card in her wallet that was still usable. Money was tight and bills weren't getting paid, but Sonya Hartiq had a grasp on destiny, and she wasn't about to let a lack of funds loosen her grip. A visit to the hair stylist was also in order along with new makeup. The good stuff this time, Este Lauder, not the cheap dollar store product she always used before. Six hundred twenty-seven dollars of debt later, Sonya was ready to rock and roll. She was taking this one to the fair for the blue ribbon.

Sonya wanted this man. Tony wanted this woman. Both were unsure if they measured up to the other's standards.

Should Tony fess up to what he was all about? Should Sonya tell Tony about the Bryan Robbins episode? Would she be horrified about his "contracting" work? Would he think she was some kind of 'slut'? They both had time to consider the consequences on their respective flights to Chicago.

Both Tony's and Sonya's flights arrived right on time. Secrets still- kept, guilt locked away for the time being. Chicago's Midway is always less congested than O'Hare on the other side of the city. Southwest airlines uses Midway as its Chicago hub and passengers astute enough to use Southwest to Chicago are generally rewarded with a more pleasant flying experience; at least as far as arrivals, departures, delays and congestion are concerned.

Tony was there waiting as Sonya walked off the departure ramp. Looking around anxiously for her love, she lit up when she spotted him standing there with that seductive smile.

She half ran, half walked directly toward him and they abandoned all modesty as they embraced and kissed on the walkway. Each were generally reserved about public displays of affection, but this moment in time was different.

After an almost full minute swaddled in Tony's arms, they walked hand in hand toward the baggage check. Tony had just a small satchel he'd checked in, but Sonya had two suitcases where she'd packed enough clothing and accessories for a two-week vacation. Ordinarily, his would have been just a "carry on," but the handgun and syringe required that he check his bag on this weekend jaunt.

Their bags came out on their respective conveyor belts without a hitch and now it was off to the hotel. Tony had booked a room at the Four Seasons in North Chicago. The cabs were lined up right outside the airport and within minutes they were transported to the arena of their fantasy Chicago weekend. For Tony, it was partially a work weekend, as he had to fulfill the contract, but that wouldn't detract from their romantic adventure.

The Four Seasons was arguably the finest hotel in Chicago proper. Located just a few blocks north of the famous "Water Tower Place" and Magnificent Mile shopping and dining mecca. Rated 5 stars and 5 diamonds, the views from the rooms overlooking Lake Michigan and the city sky light were unimaginably spectacular. Tony had reserved a one-bedroom suite.

The taxi pulled up to the hotel entrance and the valet was right there to greet them. He would take their bags and hold them until they were assigned their accommodations. A twenty-dollar tip for the taxi driver, another ten for the valet. In Chicago, if it moves, you tip it. Especially at upscale hotels.

Checking in to the hotel presented itself to be confusing for Sonya. Walking up to the desk, Tony exclaimed:

"Reservations for Mr. and Mrs. Sanders!"

"Yes sir! We have you right here. To confirm Mr. Sanders,, you've reserved a one-bedroom petite suite for the weekend?"

"That's correct"

"Excellent! May I please have a credit card for incidentals during your stay?"

"Certainly!"

Tony handed the clerk a black American Express card with the name Anthony Sanders embedded on the bottom right.

Sonya thought to herself: *"What's this about? Mr. & Mrs. Sanders?*

When she visited in Kansas City, he mentioned that he used that name professionally but, she was taken aback by the "Mr. & Mrs. Sanders thing. She'd ask him what was going on when they got to their room.

Just like his airline tickets, Tony wasn't about to use his real name for hotel reservations. As far as the world was concerned, Tony Messina was never there. He knew when Sonya heard the other name, she'd be asking questions. He was ready.

When they got to the room, Sonya was awestruck. She'd been in so called, upscale hotel rooms before, but nothing like this. This was breath taking. In fact, the entire venue was breath taking. Marble everywhere! Conversation pieces of artwork, sculpture and photographs in the lobby. To her, it was easily the most magnificent place on the famous Magnificent Mile.

Back to reality. She had a question for Mr. Sanders.

He knew this was coming.

"Uh Tony! Can I ask you something?"

"Of course! I bet you want to know why they called us Mr. and Mrs. Sanders!"

"Well, yes!

As I tried to explain when you came to visit, Anthony Sanders is a professional name. I use it for business. It keeps people from bugging me night and day with business calls and texts. No worries. Back in Kansas City, I'm Tony Messina again. "

"Am I married to Anthony Sanders?"

"As far as the hotel is concerned you are, and for my part, that's a great idea."

Then, there was a knock at the door. It was the bellman, delivering their luggage. Another tip and he was on his way.

"You know, it's been a long day. I'm gonna take a shower and rinse off a bit."

"That sounds great babe! Mind if I go first?"

"No! not at all! You go ahead! I have a couple of calls to make anyway. There should be a robe in the closet by the door. Just go ahead and grab one. Enjoy!"

"Once Sonya got in the bathroom, Tony listened carefully for the shower to start running. Then, he grabbed one of the burner phones from his satchel and called the number given to him by Freddy back in K.C."

"Hello?"

"Hello, is this Mr. Rogers?"

"Who's calling?"

"Howdy Doody"

"Hello Mr. Doody. Listen carefully. Your business contact's name is Jackie Marsala. Every Saturday he goes out to the Green Mill lounge in North Chicago with his girlfriend. You'll recognize him. He's a short guy, about five foot five, wears a black, wide brimmed hat. Never takes it off in public. He and his girlfriend get there early, like seven o'clock. They like to sit in a booth, listen to jazz music. The place is like wall to wall people by nine, so however you're most comfortable meeting him. Give him my regards. Goodbye"

Sonya was still in the shower when Mr. Rogers abruptly hung up. Tony didn't ask why Mr. Marsala was on the hit list. They wouldn't have told him anyway and he didn't care. Just do the job, get paid, and get the hell out of Chicago. It's not that there weren't plenty of mob thugs in Chicago who could have made the hit themselves, but these things were better done by a faraway professional. Almost impossible to trace, clean. No muss, no fuss.

Tony heard the shower turned off. His turn. He reached in his satchel for a change of clothes, laid them on the bed and grabbed the other bathrobe from the closet.

He'd been to Chicago a few times in the past. Not always for business. There was an intimate little restaurant over on the west side. Their specialty was fondue served in a private booth, closed off by individual curtains. The wine list was exquisitely extensive. Tony had been there before, some time ago. He'd take Sonya there tonight if she was up for it. Tomorrow, they'd visit a Jazz Club called the Green Mill Lounge.

Sonya emerged from the bathroom. "Your turn Mr. Sanders"

Tony managed a knowing smile and dutifully made his own way to the bathroom and closed the door behind him.

Sonya's hair was dripping wet. *"Damn it! I forgot my hair drier!"*

Like most upscale hotels, there was one in the bathroom, but Sonya didn't want to interrupt Tony by barging in, but she needed to get a blow drier.

On the way back to the bathroom, Sonya noticed Tony's bag was unzipped and opened.

Not thinking, Tony had unpacked the gun and syringe and laid them beside his bag on the bed.

"What is that? Is that a gun? Why would he have a gun?

Sonya didn't know what to think. First, they're Mr. & Mrs. Sanders, then, there was the gun. This was getting weird. Should she ask him about it? She needed to think.

"Wow! That was refreshing! Say Sony! I know a great restaurant over on the West Side. Would you be in the mood for fondue for dinner tonight!"

"Huh? Oh! Sure Tony, that sounds terrific! I haven't had fondue in forever!"

Great! You're gonna love this place! I'll make reservations for 6:30, that ok with you?

"Sure! Perfect! If you're finished in there, I need to blow dry my hair."

Go ahead sweetie. I'll just sit and watch TV for a bit.

Looking in the mirror while she dried her hair, Sonya thought to herself:

"Should I be worried? This is all so wonderful, but what's that gun about?"

The day went on with mostly small talk between them. At six, they headed downstairs to the hotel entrance. The Door Man hailed the next cab waiting in line for passengers. Once again, in the Chicago tradition, Tony afforded the Door Man his gratuity.

The Cabbie would be next. Using the Uber app would somehow have been a little easier but having an Uber driver, pick you up in front of this 5-star hotel in a beat-up clunker was tantamount to going to the prom in a tux and dirty sneakers with white athletic socks.

"Take us to Gejas Café over on West Armitage please! You know where that is?"

"Yes sir, I've been there many times!"

"Sweetie, I'm sure you'll love this place. I think it's the most romantic in all the city."

The Cabbie chimed in . . .

"You're husband's right ma'am! You're gonna love it."

Of course, Tony wasn't her husband, but neither said anything to the Cab Driver. They'd just let it be.

Pulling up to the restaurant, Sonya was somewhat perplexed. There was a black, wrought iron fence with a gate that opened to steps leading down into the restaurant below street level.

There was nothing like that in Omaha, or even Kansas City as far as she knew. But sub street level restaurants were common in cities like Chicago and New York.

Once inside, the gentle music of live flamenco guitar permeated the atmosphere. Sonya was becoming overwhelmed.

"Reservations for Sanders r please"

"Certainly! Welcome Mr.Sanders! We've reserved a private booth for you in the guitar section. Will that accommodate your preferences sir?"

"Yes, absolutely. And thank you!"

"Very good sir! Ramon' will take you to your table."

And again, as protocol demanded, Tony handed the Maitre' D a twenty.

For Sonya the whole atmosphere was dream like. Surreal. A private, curtained booth, gold, linen tablecloth, and a fondue apparatus sitting in the middle with a flame underneath dancing to the classical guitar playing just a few steps away. This was as close to heaven as she was going to get on this earth. She wondered how many times Tony had been here before, and with whom.

Their waiter was beyond attentive. Dressed to fit the romantic environment. White linen jacket, black bow tie, smartly pressed trousers over gleamingly shined, black lace up shoes.

"Good evening! My name is Carlos. Shall we have a beverage before dinner tonight?"

"Yes Carlos! I'll have a glass of Stag's Leap Artemis, Cabernet Sauvignon, and the lady will have a glass of your Moscato."

"Excellent choices sir. I'll return shortly with your order"

"I hope that's what you wanted Sony! I guess I should have asked."

"No! No Tony! That's perfect. I love Moscato! You know me well."

"Well, I want tonight to be special for you! I want you to be glad you came here with me."

"It's absolutely dreamy Tony. But you need to know I'd be happy anywhere, as long as you're close by."

The evening did not disappoint. It was a sumptuous fondue dinner experience, with cheeses, beef, Australian lobster and chocolate; complemented by the most palatable wine and delivered by Carlos spontaneously as they finished each course.

Though she was intensely curious, Sonya decided not to bring up the gun she had found beside Tony's satchel earlier in the day. That could wait. There was still plenty of weekend left and popping this glorious romance bubble wasn't going to be on the agenda.

Three hours and $265 later, they were back in the hotel room. The night was still young, and the pent up, breathless anticipation of the other's touch was uncaged as they fell onto the bed. No need to pull down the bedspread or even disrobe. Tonight, would be a savage pleasure. Discarding all sexual inhibitions to accommodate the intense lust they shared for one another. Clothing unfurled, buttons ripped off and away in all directions, buckles disengaged, zippered barriers to entry liberated. It was over almost as soon as it began. He released his seed inside her. She orgasmed in concert as they became one in a furious, violent carnal dance. And then, satiated with the warm afterglow, they collapsed into each other and a wine induced sleep came over them. It was the indefectible conclusion to an evening of rare emotion.

Tomorrow, he had a job to do.

CHAPTER 19

"No Worries!"

Saturday morning, 8:35 a.m. the amorous couple awakened to a knock on the door.

"HOUSEKEEPING!"

They had forgotten to put the "Do not disturb" card on the door last night.

Tony got up out of bed and half stumbled into the living room.

"We're still here! Can you come back later please?"

A soft woman's voice answered from the outside hallway: "Certainly Sir! Thank you!"

With all the commotion, Sonya got up out of bed as well. Tony turned to her as she walked into the adjoining living room. "Well! Whaddya say Babe! Ready for breakfast? What's your pleasure? I'll order it up!"

Sonya was all in. "Bacon, eggs over easy, hash browns extra crispy, rye toast dry, butter on the side, orange juice and of course coffee!"

When he spoke to the room service kitchen, Sonya could hear that he had amazingly memorized exactly what she told him plus a bagel, cream cheese, scrambled eggs and bacon. It would be ready in twenty minutes.

When the food arrived, it was presented like a work of art. Everything on china plate, linen wrapped silver ware, and a rose in a petite vase strategically placed to perfectly accentuate the ensemble.

Tony complimented the server. "It looks terrific! Thank you, sir." There was that polite, congenial Tony Messina that Sonya knew. Always nice to people.

"Well, this looks delicious! But I have to say, not as delicious as you were last night"

"Aww, that's sweet babe. But it's all so easy with you"

"Let's eat! I'm famished!"

Between them, they devoured their breakfast in record time. When they finished, Sonya decided this was a good time to ask about the gun on the bed. She noticed that it wasn't there this morning. She leaned back on the sofa, crossed her arms and spoke up.

"Uh... honey, I need to ask you about something."

"Again? OK! What's up Babe?"

"Yesterday... "

Interrupting her in mid-sentence, Tony interjected.

"Yesterday was a slice of heaven Babe."

"Yes, Babe, it was, but something happened."

"Happened? What happened?"

"Well, I don't mean <u>happened</u> exactly. I mean I accidentally discovered something."

"Really? Well, what was it?"

"Well, after I took my shower yesterday morning, I came out of the bathroom before I dried my hair. You went right in after me, and I didn't want to interrupt you. But, then I decided you wouldn't mind if I just came in and grabbed the hair drier. Anyway, as I walked to the bathroom, there was a gun sitting on the bed next to your satchel!"

Tony smiled and grinned at her.

"Sony, I wish you had said something yesterday instead of worrying about it all this time. I have a permit for that gun Babe! Specifically, what's called a 'Concealed Carry Permit.' Chicago can be a dangerous town. I brought it with me just in case we ran into trouble. Here! Let me show you my permit ID."

With that, he went over to his wallet sitting on the nightstand in the bedroom. He pulled out the ID and showed it to Sonya.

It sure looked official. Tony's picture and all on the ID. She didn't bother to ask about the bubble wrapped syringe next to the pistol. It was probably insulin or something and she was embarrassed enough about the gun episode.

"So! We good Babe? You ok with it?"

"I'm so sorry Tony. I don't know what to say. I should have asked you about it yesterday when you came out of the bathroom. I'm just afraid of guns. I've heard so many stories. I've never even seen a real gun in person."

"It's ok Babe. I understand! Here! Would you like to look at it close up?"

"No! No! That's ok. Thank you for understanding Tony, I love you so much!"

"I'm just glad you asked me about it. Now that that's out of the way, let's enjoy the day.

You know they don't call this the Magnificent Mile for nothing! We can walk around, window shop, pick up lunch somewhere later. There's a million first class restaurants right up the street. Maybe we can get you a new outfit for tonight. Remember! Jazz at the Green Mill Lounge!"

To say Sonya was relieved would be a gross understatement. She should have known there was a plausible explanation. She didn't like guns, or being near them, but she knew Tony was right. Watching television, she'd seen and heard about all the gangland shootings in Chicago.

Anyway, she felt completely safe with Tony right beside her. He was more man than anyone she'd ever met in her 32 years on the planet. The weekend just kept getting better.

CHAPTER 20

"Goodbye Mr. Marsala"

Saturday afternoon was exciting, romantic and relaxing all at the same time. They walked over to the Water Tower Place; a 74-story skyscraper with more than a hundred shops and restaurants. Tony insisted Sonya try on some things at an upscale women's clothing store called Aritiza. Sonya didn't want him spending money on her like that, but still, they walked out with almost $800 worth of new tops, jeans and jewelry. Lunch was a casual burger at a place called Mity Nice Bar and Grill right in Water Tower.

By the time they returned to the hotel, it was almost 6 O'clock. They were already dressed appropriately enough for the Green Mill, so no need to go through it all over again. Virtually every restaurant on the Mag Mile, and there were many, had nightly Jazz entertainment, and Sonya wondered why they would go all the way out North, but Tony insisted it was the perfect entertainment spot. Sonya would love it.

Their cab headed North around 6:30. Didn't want to get there late, the place filled up fast. When they arrived 30 minutes later, Sonya was surprised to see that it looked pretty much like any other bar back in South Omaha. Certainly not an upscale neighborhood.

But the Green Mill Lounge is a storied place. Behind the bar is a shrine to the famous mobster Al Capone, who used to frequent the Green Mill in the '30s. At one time, Al Jolson and Billy Holiday performed there on stage. The inside still had a 1930's ambience, including a big band stage, left over from the roaring twenties when singers would use megaphones.

This is where Tony Messina would do his work. His mark, Jackie Marsala was already there sitting in a booth at the back end of the bar with a young blonde, late twenties, literally dripping in diamond and gold jewelry. Jackie was easy to spot. Just as Mr. Rogers said, he was wearing that wide brimmed hat. He looked to be in his mid-fifties. He was facing the back of the bar towards the stage. The woman was on the other side of the booth facing her paramour and the entrance.

Tony had both his handgun and the syringe in his jacket but wasn't sure which he would use to accomplish the task. There was already a jazz group on stage by 7 but, the main entertainment wouldn't start until 9. Sonya was kind of taken aback by the whole thing. Especially when Tony told her all about the history of the place and showed her the Al Capone memorial behind the bar.

They seated themselves in a booth along the wall across from the bar and a little way from the stage.

The place was starting to fill up. By 8:30 it was full and by 9 it was standing room only. In fact, the place became so packed, if one were inclined to be uncomfortable in crowds, you had just placed yourself in claustrophobia hell. One wouldn't expect it in a retro Jazz bar but, on most nights it was full of twenty somethings, shoulder to shoulder and ready to party.

This all worked to Tony's advantage. He could feign a need to go to the bathroom to Sonya, then walk up to Jackie Marsala's booth and do what he came for. He could hardly see the booth through the crowded room but caught a glimpse of Jackie's girlfriend heading for the ladies room. This was his chance. From his jacket pocket lying next to him in the booth, he clandestinely exported the syringe, wrapped a napkin around it and excused himself to Sonya for his own bathroom run. But first, he would take a detour.

Tony worked his way through the crowd, bouncing off individuals and up to the booth where Jackie Marsala was sitting, himself trying to look through the audience of bodies at the band on the stage. He couldn't see or didn't notice Tony standing right behind him.

Tony stealthily removed the cap off the syringe, still wrapped in the napkin, and stuck it firmly into the neck of his prey. 20mm of the lethal Carfentanil flowed directly into his artery. A dazed Jackie Marsala looked up at his assassin and then slumped forward onto the booth table, his wide brimmed hat knocked sideways. There was no antidote for this, he would die in minutes, if not sooner.

No one noticed the event. All eyes were on the band on stage. Tony took the now empty syringe, down below his waist, carefully replaced the cap and made his way to the men's room. Once there, he wiped it down to remove any trace of fingerprints and quietly tossed it in the men's room trash. It would soon be covered with paper towels and emptied by maintenance in the morning.

Outside the men's room a high-pitched scream pierced the entire establishment. It was Jackie Marsala's girlfriend. As she returned to their booth, finding Jackie's head lying on the table, white foam emanating from his mouth, she went into a frenzied panic, punctuated by her howling shrieks. All eyes turned toward their booth.

Pushing through the crowd, Tony made his way to Sonya.

"What happened?"

"I don't know! A woman up there near the stage just started screaming!"

A young man standing next to them said: "I think some old guy up there just had a heart attack"

"Oh, that poor man! Tony! Maybe we should leave!"

"That's a good idea Sony, let's go outside, I'll call a cab."

By the time they got back to the hotel, Sonya had collected herself. All she could talk about on the drive home was "That poor man! Do you think he had a heart attack? I hope he didn't die!"

Tony thought: *"Oh, he died alright!"* But comforted Sonya.

"Honey I'm sure he survived! The ambulance was there before we left! He'll be ok."

"I sure hope so Babe. What a night!"

"Let's have a drink at the bar before we go upstairs, we can calm down a little."

After they ordered their drinks in the bar, Tony excused himself again to make a bathroom pit stop. There, he pulled out another of the burner phones, called "Mr. Rogers" and informed him the package was delivered, then hung up abruptly. Once again, he disposed of the burner phone in the Men's room trash. He assumed Mr. Rogers did the same on his end.

Coming out to their table in the bar, they bemoaned the fact that their flights would be leaving in the morning. When would she see him again? He assured her it would be sooner rather than later. But after the unfortunate event at the Green Mill and the emotional ripples afterward, their conversation took a decidedly somber tone.

"Let's go to bed Tony. I want to be next to you tonight"

They both slept well in each other's arms. Once again, Tony woke up before Sonya. He had one more call to make. It was to Freddy In K.C., the man who arranged the entire assassination. He slipped out the bed as quietly as possible, tip toed into the living room and pulled the third burner phone out of his bag. He dialed the final number given to him when he left Kansas City.

As he went out of the bedroom, without knowing it, he awakened Sonya. She laid there, not yet wanting to get out from under the covers. She could hear Tony speaking in muffled tones.

"Hello Micky Mouse! This is Donald Duck. The package was delivered last night!"

With that, he hung up and tossed the burner phone in the trash can by the sofa.

Sonya thought: *"That was weird!"* Then she had an epiphany. *"Tony was supposed to be here for a contractor meeting. But he never spent a moment away from me to do any kind of business. Something's wrong."* Sonya got out of bed, put on her robe and went out in the living room to confront him.

"Oh! Good morning Babe! Did I wake you?"

"Tony! What's going on?"

"What do you mean?"

"I mean, I heard you on the phone this morning, calling Micky Mouse about some package! Mickey Mouse? You're calling Mickey Mouse and YOU'RE Donald Duck? You're keeping something from me Tony, I don't care what it is, I don't. I love you unconditionally Tony! But please don't hide from me. Tell me what's going on!"

Tony laughed out loud. He sounded genuine. He wanted badly to tell her the truth, but he saw how upset she got just thinking Marsala had a heart attack. He couldn't bring himself to tell her he murdered the guy.

"Oh! You heard the Donald Duck thing! Me and Bob have this on-going joke He calls me Donald Duck and I call him Mickey Mouse. He's real wine snob and can't get it this certain bottle where he lives. I sent it off to him from

K.C. before I left. I was just double checking to see if his package arrived. It was supposed to be there yesterday, but I didn't want to call him last night."

"Babe, you have to trust me. You have to trust me! There isn't anything you can tell me that would make me turn away from you. Just please tell me. First there was the Mr & Mrs. Sanders thing, then the gun and now Donald Duck?"

"I know, but honestly Babe, I've explained it all to you! Let's not ruin this beautiful weekend worrying about trivial things that mean nothing."

"I know you're right Tony. I'm so sorry. I'm just worried. Our relationship is so important to me."

Tony hated the deception but, this was not the time.

"It's just as important to me sweetie. I would never do anything to hurt you."

With that, things calmed down a little. After breakfast, they put their luggage together and headed out for the airport right on time. She was flying back to Omaha, and he was heading back to Kansas City. Different gates, different times. Tony accompanied her to her concourse. When they got to her gate, he handed her a bulky, sealed envelope.

"This is for you Babe! Please call me as soon as you're able. IF you're able. I miss you already."

Sonya was confused. But her hand opened instinctively to accept it. *"What could this be?"*

Tony bent over and kissed her forehead. Teary eyed himself, he said nothing else but walked away toward his own flight.

Once on board the plane, Sonya opened the envelope. Inside was a bundle of one hundred-dollar bills. It looked like thousands. In fact, it was five thousand dollars, exactly half of Tony's pay for making the hit.

The gift embarrassed her. She certainly needed the money, but accepting it was hard. Still, she stuck it back in her purse and sat back, wishing she had a Xanax or something like it to calm her nerves. It had been a Cinderella weekend, but she was uneasy about some things.

CHAPTER 21

"I know someone!"

Monday. The entire weekend went by and Bryan could not connect with Sara. It wasn't that he didn't try. He called her a couple of dozen times. Texted more than that. Sunday night, he drove by the house. Lights off. Nobody home. And now, Monday's alarm clock went off on his fourth morning's stay at the Holiday Inn Express.

He was up late last night. Just sitting in the hotel room, staring at the TV, fretting. Not really watching what was on. Ordinarily, if he could break away from home on a Sunday night, he'd head straight for the bars, see if some stray was out and about.

But not last night. Last night, he just wanted his wife back. His family back. If he could just talk to her, he'd find a way to charm himself back into the fold. And he swore to himself and his God that he'd never play again. But Bryan Robbins was kidding himself. Womanizing was embedded in his DNA. Once a player, always a player, and Sara wasn't on the other end of his attempted communications.

At least he had most of his clothes and toiletries. There were still some of his things at the house and he was glad about that. It would give him an excuse to come over and pick up the rest. Then, maybe he could talk with her.

That was unlikely. Sara was already in revenge mode. Last week, she had gone to bed with her attorney moments after Bryan was made to leave the house. She had managed to turn her love for Bryan off like a light switch. She was surprised at how easy it was.

It was the longest weekend of Bryan's life. Hours upon hours of just sitting and calling, calling and texting and in between trying to watch TV in his hotel room to keep his mind off this dilemma.

He made it to work at the advertising agency around 10 a.m. Should he tell anyone about what happened or, just keep it quiet? After all it was probably just a false alarm. In his mind, Sara wouldn't really divorce him, would she? He just needed her to sit down and talk. Good luck with that.

"Hey Boss Man!'

There he was, good ole' Stanley. Never far away from his hero and mentor.

"What's up Bryan? You look stressed!"

"Uh, I had a bad fight with Sara over the weekend." There, he'd spilled the beans already.

"Something serious?"

"Nah! Just a disagreement. Say Stan, where's a dry cleaner around here? I need to get some things pressed"

"There's a MAX I Walker over in a strip mall just off 114th and Davenport. That work for you?"

"That'll do. Thanks."

Usually, Bryan would stand and talk with Stan but today was different. He made a beeline over to his office and shut the door.

Stan figured something was up but decided this wasn't a good time to press the issue.

"Musta' been a hell of a fight!"

Lunch time came and, as usual, Bryan, Stan, and Joe Henke all headed off to Charleston's for some chow and a couple of drinks to wash it down. Bryan wasn't his usual talkative self. The others sensed something wasn't quite right. After he downed his Chicken Pietro and two Johnny Walker Reds, Stan announced he'd better get back. Joe took off right behind him, leaving Bryan sitting there in a booth by himself. Just then, Mike Holland walked in. He immediately spotted Bryan sitting alone and walked over to him.

"Lunch by yourself today Bryan?"

"Oh! Hi Mike! No, the other guys went back to work. I decided to sit here a little longer."

Mike Holland worked for KMTV 3, the CBS affiliate in the city. He'd called on Bryan occasionally to pitch some new promotion the station had to offer. He was more of an acquaintance than a friend, but Bryan was familiar enough with him to invite him to sit.

"You here alone Mike?"

"Yean, just thought I'd come in a get a quick bite between appointments."

"Well, sit down. I'll signal the waitress!"

"Well, ok! That's nice of you Bryan. How's things going?"

"Hmm ... a little rough lately."

"Rough? How's that? Business good?"

"Business is terrific. I'm just having some issues at home."

Somehow, it was easier to talk to a pseudo stranger than to friends.

"Yeah, my wife filed for divorce last week."

"Jesus! You've been married awhile! What happened?"

"She thinks I was running around on her."

That was no surprise to Mike Holland, . Everyone knew Bryan was a player. In fact, most advertising execs in the city were players, married or not. Mike decided to ask anyway.

"Well, were you?"

"No! But some bitch called her and told her I was. I swear I'd kill her if I could."

"Who? Your wife or the other one?"

Bryan smirked.

"Both of 'em! Lol"

"Wow!"

"I mean it. I'd have that bitch killed if I could. Sara's big time pissed at me."

"Mad enough to divorce you, I guess"

"Bingo! Anyway, she won't even talk to me. All because that woman called and gave me up."

"Anybody I know?"

"Nah, she's not in advertising. I met her one night at a bar"

"Hmmm ... you mean the lounge over on Pacific Street where that guy was strangled?"

"Yeah, that's it."

"Well, I thought you said you didn't have sex with her!"

"I didn't! I just met her. Had a couple of drinks. I mean, I hit on her a little, but nothing happened. She wasn't even that hot! How a person could just ruin somebody's life like that I don't know."

"Well, don't worry about it Bryan, it'll all work out."

"I hope so. I'm living at the Holiday Inn Express in the meantime."

"Oh! That's harsh! That's when you hire hit men"

"Yeah! Really!"

"in fact, I heard about a guy who did that. I don't know if the story's real, but there's this guy I know named Bobby Jenkins. He swears he's connected to those types in Kansas City. But the guys a big blow hard, I think he just wants people to think he's some kind of cloak and dagger dangerous."

"Ok Mike. Anyway, I better get back to work. If you have any attractive programming packages, come see me sometime. I'll listen."

"Ok Bryan. Thanks! Have a good day!

Mike Holland seemed genuine when he talked about this Jenkins guy. The more he thought about it, the more the whole idea seemed plausible. That is, if there really *was* a hit man connection.

"Do they still call them hit men? Do they still exist? Or, is that just a movie plot? Bryan wasn't sure."

As the day moved on, it was all Bryan could think about. He decided to call Mike Holland one more time for a business lunch. Tomorrow if possible.

CHAPTER 22

"Wouldn't hurt to call!"

Deposition day was harsh for Bryan Robbins. As he drove up to Sara's attorney's office he noticed his soon to be ex-wife was arriving at the same time, in the same car as her lawyer. They looked cozy. Apparently, they'd had lunch together.

About that time, Bryan's counsel pulled up next to him. This whole miserable fiasco was getting expensive. Already he'd paid his lawyer the required $5000 retainer. Supposed to be the best divorce counsel in the city.

"We'll see" he thought as he watched him exit his Mercedes coup. *"I'll probably wind up paying for her attorney as well, that's the way it usually goes in these matters. You pay for the weapon they use to kill you."*

"Hey Bryan! Good to see you! Ready to go?"

Bryan replied in a disgusted, defeated voice: "Yeah, sure! Can't wait!"

"Well, it'll all be ok, let's go inside and get this over with."

The deposition lasted about 90 minutes. Court stenographer, the whole shebang. Sara's attorney grilled Bryan.. Asking about all the infidelities, the STD he brought home to his wife, his finances, insurance and more. For his part, Bryan's attorney objected to a good bit of the inquiries and was as firm and caustic towards Sara as he could be without violating protocol.

When it was all over, Bryan spoke with his attorney out in the hallway, while Sara and counsel retired to his office. Bryan wondered what they'd be doing in there.

"It'll be ok Bryan. You just relax. It's what you pay me for. I've been down this road with disgruntled wives a thousand times. They come out swinging at first, but after a bit, we'll hand her a reality sandwich that divorce isn't all it's cracked up to be. She might even ask you to come back to her; but I need to ask, did you *really* give her an STD?"

The truth being too humiliating, Bryan decided to tell his attorney a little white lie. What did it matter anyway?

"No! it was a urinary tract infection! My doctor even said so!"

"Would he testify to that in court?"

"I don't know, He's a friend of mind so ... "

"Why don't you call him and ask. It would be good to have him testify if that comes up"

"Ok, I'll do that."

Feeling completely defeated, Bryan skipped the bar scene and went straight to his now seemingly permanent hotel room at the Holiday Inn Express.

He'd better call Doctor Steve.

"Hello?"

"Steve! It's Bryan Robbins! I'm sorry to call you at home."

"That's ok Bryan! What's up bud?"

"Well, believe it or not, my wife's divorcing me."

"Oh Damn! I'm sorry buddy!"

"Well, she's suing me for everything Steve! She's going to testify in court that I gave her an STD!"

"Oh!"

"Well, you know it was just a urinary tract infection, right?"

"Well, yes, I guess so."

"Bryan! I can't do that pal. You have to leave me out of this! I could lose my license!"

"Well, you gave me medication for a urinary tract infection"

"I really don't remember doing that Bryan.. That's it! Listen! I gotta go! Talk later!"

And Dr. Steve abruptly hung up the phone.

Talking to himself, Bryan mumbled: *"Well, that settles that. Nice friend. Guess I can't blame him. That Hartiq bitch started all this. What if Sara subpoenas her? She'll tell it all in court! I'm gonna call Mike Holland, he said he knew somebody. I have to do SOMETHING!"*

CHAPTER 23

"The Connection"

Bryan called and set up a lunch meeting with Mike Holland for the next day under the guise of maybe having some advertising business for him. But his real motive was to see if this 'mob connection thing' was legitimate.

He was sitting in one of the booths that sat parallel to the bar at Charleston's. It was relatively private there, and Bryan was anticipating the most private of conversations. He actually would have preferred an office meeting but didn't want to spook Mike by making it seem like cloak and dagger stuff. The stools that circled the bar were just a few feet away from the booths, but they sat facing away. It would suffice for privacy. He'd be speaking in code anyway.

It was almost 1 p.m. and Bryan had decided to get up and leave, as he was sure his friend had either forgotten their meeting or just decided to stand him up, when he came rushing through the door, spotted Bryan and half ran over to his booth.

"I am soooo sorry Bryan! I got hung up on a story for the 6 o'clock news and had to finish the video before I could leave."

"It's ok bro. I figured you forgot or something. But I'm glad you're here. What can I get you to drink?"

"Johnny Walker Red and water tall will work fine. So, what's up Bryan?"

"Well, as fate would have it. I think I have a buy schedule for you with one of my clients. Not a big buy, just about five thousand, but I thought you'd appreciate it. I didn't want to talk about it over the phone, thought we'd have lunch."

"That's great pal! I can use the business! When do you want to start the schedule?"

"Hmm, not till the end of the month, but I'll need you to get me some good times. Thirty-second ads in the evening news."

"Consider it done my friend."

Now, Bryan could set the bait.

Say Mike, you remember last time we met, you said you knew a guy who knew a guy who did things?"

"You mean that Kansas City mob thing?"

Just then, the waitress came over. Bryan became visibly irritated by the intrusion in the conversation, but she was simply doing her job.

"Yes! Please get my friend a Johnny Walker Red and water tall and bring me another Chivas."

"Yeah I think so. You said he was connected somehow. I was talking about it to a friend who needs something like that, and I was wondering if you could get me the name and phone number. Obviously, I don't know anyone in that line of work myself."

"Well, sure! I can get it for you Bryan, but you'll have to be careful how you talk to these people. What kind of work does your friend want done?"

"You know, I'm not real sure, but he wants to keep it quiet."

The waitress returned all too soon, "Here you are sir!" Bryan's irritation was obvious.

"Ok! Ok! Just run a tab please!"

"Certainly sir, I'm sorry I interrupted."

"It's ok! Thank you for the drinks. Goodbye now!"

Mike Holland didn't like this. The waitress couldn't win. If she took too long to bring the drinks, he'd have been even more irritated. This was rude. He frequented this place often and didn't need the help to consider him a jerk by osmosis.

"I apologize Mike, I've just been really stressed lately. I told you things aren't good at home."

"It's ok Bryan, but don't apologize to me, apologize to the girl who brought the drinks."

"Yeah! I will! When she comes back. Anyway, who is this guy? Can you tell me how to reach him?"

"Well, like I told you, I know a guy who says he knows a guy. You can call him and if you mention me, he'll probably give you some contact information. I don't know if he was just bragging or if he really knows someone, but you can try.

"So, you can you give me his number?"

"Yes, but whatever happens, leave me out of it from here on out."

"That's no problem Mike. You know me."

That was the problem. Mike Holland knew him too well.

Once again, the waitress returned.

"Everything alright here gentlemen?"

"Uh..yeah! You want another one Mike?"

"No! That's alright."

"Then just bring the bill."

"Right away sir!"

"Bryan! I thought you were going to apologize!"

"Ahh, she'll get over it. Wasn't that big a deal was it?"

"I guess not. Ok, well, thanks again for the business. I'll text you that guy's number. His name's Bobby. You can take it from there.

Even before Bryan treated the waitress so rudely, Mike Holland had misgivings about turning over his friend's number. It was a side of Bryan Robbins he hadn't seen before. They weren't even friends really; he and Mike Holland just knew each other casually. Anyway, Bobby probably didn't really know anyone from the mob. Just some drunken bragging over a couple of beers.

It didn't take long for Bryan to find out. Minutes after Mike left the restaurant, Bryan paid the bill, left a dollar tip and went out to his car to call this Bobby fellow.

"Hello?"

"Hi! Is this Bobby?"

"Uh . . . yeah, who's this?"

"Uh . . . Bobby, my name's Sam. I got your number from Mike Holland,. He said you might know somebody in Kansas City who might be able to do something for me."

"Mike gave you my number?"

"Yes! He said you might be able to help me!"

"Well, possibly. I know some people, but how do I know who you are?"

"Like I said, I'm a friend of Mike's, he gave me your number."

"Tell you what, I'll give you a number of a guy, but I don't want to know what you're about and don't mention my name or anything about me ok?

"Ok! Sure!"

"I mean it pal, I'll give you a number, but that's it. Leave me out of whatever you're doing."

"Ok! Ok! I promise!"

"Alright. When you call ask for Freddy. After that, the ball's in your court. Remember, don't mention my name."

Bobby gave Bryan the number and repeated one more time not to mention his name. Bryan decided not to make another call from his car. He'd wait till he got back to his hotel room to call this Freddy guy.

Once in his room, he dialed the Kansas City number: 814-...-....

"Heelllo"

"Hi, uh, is this Freddy?"

"Who's this?"

"Hi Freddy, my name's Sam, Bobby in Omaha, told me to call you, that you might be able to help me with a problem."

Even though Bobby asked three times and made him promise to keep him and his name out of it, Bryan Robbins paid no attention to that promise. He blurted it out immediately.

"Bobby in Omaha? I don't know anybody named Bobby in Omaha! What's this about?"

"Well, Bobby said you sometimes help people who're in trouble."

"Sometimes. What's your name again?"

"My name's Sam. I live in Omaha."

"Ok Sam, give me a number I'll call you and we can talk."

"Ok!"

Bryan was almost sorry he called. This guy sounded like the real thing. He gave Freddy his number and Freddy pulled one of the burner phones he kept nearby and minutes later, he called Bryan back.

"Hello?"

"Hello! Is this Sam?"

"Uh . . . yes! This is Sam"

"Sam, this is a guy you called earlier. Why don't you tell me exactly what you want?"

"Well, I need someone out of my life."

"Ok, what makes you think I can help you with that?"

"I'm not sure. Can you help me?"

"It depends on what you need. We'll have to talk more. Here's what I want you to do. I want you to buy two burner phones at a convenience store. You know what those are?"

"Uh, not really."

"Ok, those are disposable phones. You can buy them at almost any convenience store. Call me at this number from one of those phones and give me the number of the other.

Then throw the first phone away in a dumpster somewhere and I'll call you back on the second phone. Got it?"

"Yessir!"

"OK! Go and do that now. Call me at 8 p.m. tonight at this number. We'll talk."

"Alright sir, I'll do that"

Bryan went out to the nearest convenience store and bought two burner phones, $28.50 each. He put in two different numbers in each of the phones and waited until 8 p.m. Then he called Freddy, or whomever he was.

"Hello?"

"Hello Sir! This is Sam"

"Alright Sam. Dispose of this phone and give me the number of your other phone."

"Bryan gave him the second number"

"Ok, I'll call you back. Remember to destroy this one. My name is Johnny Speck."

"Freddy then picked up another of his burners and called the new number"

"Hu ... hello!"

"Hello, Sam? This is Johnny Speck"

"Yes Mr. Speck?"

"Do you want something special?"

"Well, yes!"

"How special?"

"Uh ... I'm not sure."

"Well, there's different kinds of special. And different prices for different specials."

"I'm sure."

"Well, special prices start at $5k, depending on how special you want. Can you pay that?"

"Yessir!"

"Ok, we need to meet. Can you come to K.C. this weekend?"

"I think so. What day? Where?"

"Saturday! Keep this phone. Be here by 2 p.m., someone will call you, tell you where to meet. Ok?"

"Yessir"

"Ok ... we'll see you then. Bring cash. At least $10k. We'll call you at 2 p.m."

"I thought you said five thousand?"

"I said prices start at $5k. We don't know what you want, we need to talk in person"

"Alright then. 2 p.m. Saturday, I'm in KC. Someone will call, right?"

"Right. See you then"

Freddy Cosenta hung up abruptly. He wasn't sure if this Sam was legitimate, but he'd know when he meets him.

The Feds all have a look about them. He'll know. He mentioned Bobby. *"Who the Hell was Bobby?"* Anyway, he'd find out.

CHAPTER 24

"Who's Bobby?"

Almost immediately after the phone conversation with Freddy, Bryan began to regret that he even made the call. He wanted Sonya to pay for what she'd done to him and his family but having her killed might be going too far.

He considered just not showing up in Kansas City, but his first phone call was from a legitimate number, these people would probably have an easy time finding him and then he'd have to answer a lot of questions, presumably to the Kansas City mob.

And so, he found himself sitting in a McDonalds parking lot on I-29 just outside the city limits waiting for his burner phone to ring. It was 1:38 p.m. He considered it would be better to arrive early than late. These weren't the kind of people you messed with. Beside him in the car was an envelope with 5 thousand cash. It occurred to Bryan that it didn't look like a lot of money when it was packaged that way.

The "Freddy" or "Mr. Speck" guy told him to bring $10k but, he couldn't get that much in a short time. He hoped he could pay the first five thousand now, and the rest later.

Even though he was expecting it, it half startled Bryan when the phone rang at exactly 2 p.m. These guys didn't fool around.

"Hello"

"Is this Sam"

"Uh . . . yes!"

"Sam, my name is Porky, are you in K.C.?"

"Yes! Yes, I am!"

"Ok, listen carefully to me. I want you to drive to Harrah's Hotel and Casino in North Kansas City. Come into the front lobby. You'll see a man in a black, camel hair sports coat with a yellow tie. Walk up to him and ask him if he knows where the buffet is located. Got it?"

"Yes! Yes, I do! Black sport coat, yellow tie, where's the buffet?"

"Go there now."

"Porky" hung up abruptly.

Bryan was perplexed. *"Did he just assume I knew where that Casino is? Well, Google Maps will get me there. I better get moving."*

The casino was close to where Bryan had parked his car. He could see the big "Harrah's" sign from the exit off I-29. As he drove up to the front of the Hotel, he decided to pull his vehicle into a "self-parking" space. No need to draw attention from a Valet.

Just then, for the first time since he made the phone call, it occurred to him that this whole fiasco might be a sting, like the ones you see on those TV reality shows. *"Anyway,"* he thought,

"I didn't really say anything specifically, AND surely they wouldn't make me jump through all those hoops with the phones and such."

There he was, standing in the lobby a short way from the front desk. The man in the sport coat with the yellow tie. He looked unremarkable. Just your average Joe, standing there. Just as instructed Bryan walked up to him and asked, "Excuse me sir! Do you know where the buffet is located?"

"Oh! Why sure! Tell you what, it's a little hard to find if you don't know your way around. Why don't I just take you there? Just follow me."

The man didn't wait for an answer. He just began walking toward the hallway with Bryan in tow right behind him. They never made it to the buffet restaurant, instead the man led Bryan to the elevators. Earlier that day, out of caution, Freddy had sent one of his cronies to book a room in the Hotel. If there was FBI surveillance, there was no way the Feds could bug a room that fast, or even know which room it would be.

The man in the sport coat pushed the 5th floor button. His demeanor was not at all threatening. He seemed very calm, almost gentlemanly. As they reached their floor, he motioned for Bryan Robbins to exit first. Then, without speaking a word, he quietly motioned for Bryan to follow him. They walked down the hall to room 528. The man knocked three times. One knock with a pause, then two more in rapid succession.

The door opened to reveal two rough looking characters who *did* look like mobsters, right out of "The Sopranos." At that point, Bryan wanted to just run away down the hall, but that really wasn't an option, as the black sport coat guy was now behind him and no longer looking friendly. Entering the room, the door slammed shut and, without saying anything, one of the thugs grabbed him and pulled him into the room's entry way, and Mr. Robbins was frisked, head to toe.

"What's this?"

"That's the money sir!"

"Better be. Pull it out!"

Bryan pulled the white envelope out of his jacket pocket and showed the man the cash inside.

They led him over to the coffee table, and Bryan slid the money over to the man.

"This is only $5k! We told you Ten thousand! $5k won't do it pal. What you want done is ten- large."

"Well, sir, I couldn't get that much by today. How about if you take this five- grand and the rest when the job is done. Isn't that how it works in these matters?"

"How would you know how it works? You done this before?"

"No Sir"

He was no longer anything like the guy who escorted him from the hotel lobby. That amateur move Bryan Robbins made just irritated the man in the black jacket.

"What! you trying to pimp me? Who are you? You have a wire?"

"What?"

"You heard me! Are you wired? Unbutton your shirt! Let's see your chest"

"Damn!"

"NOW!"

Bryan jumped a little at the thug's command, this was the real thing. He unbuttoned his shirt to reveal a bare chest. No wire. He almost wet himself. It was all so surreal. Like he was actually in some kind of gangster movie.

Without saying another word, the man got up and went into an a-joining room.

A minute later, he once again escorted Bryan deeper into the room's interior. It was a small suite with a bedroom in back and a sitting room up front. Basically, your typical Hotel Casino room. Writing desk over by the window, a sofa, coffee table, and a TV inside an armoire. Sitting in an over-stuffed armchair across from the sofa was Freddy "The Count" Cosenta, Underboss of the K.C. mob.

The two thugs led Bryan Robbins over to the sofa and each sat on either side of him. The man in the black sport coat had now disappeared.

"So! You're Sam huh?"

"Uh, yes, sir! Well, that's not really my name. I didn't want to use my real name"

"Well, that's smart Mr. Sam. So, what IS your real name?"

"Bryan sir. My name's Bryan."

"Bryan what?"

"You want my whole name?"

Freddy leaned forward in the armchair.

"Well, if we're gonna do business, don't you think I should know who I'm doin' business with?"

Bryan was tempted to ask Freddy the same thing but thought better of it. Things were getting tense.

"My name is Bryan Robbins. May I ask, are you Mr. Speck?"

"Never mind that. Tell me what you want Mr. Robbins"

"Well, I've been married for 10 years. Kids, mortgage, the whole enchilada. Now, my wife's filed for divorce."

"And?"

"Well, the reason she's filing for divorce is because some Bitch ratted me out to my wife. Told her I had sex with her."

"Did you?"

"No! She just approached my wife with some tall tale. I was in a bar, and she came over to me, started hitting on me. I was just having after work drinks with some of my co-workers and this Bitch starts in on me. She was attractive enough, but I'm married. I turned her down. I guess she doesn't handle rejection very well, cause once she found out who I was, last name and all, she got hold of my wife and made up some wild story."

"So, what do you want from us?"

"Well, I've tried but, my wife's not going to change her mind. My home, my kids, half of everything I own! I've been living at the Holiday Inn Express for weeks now. She's acting like an entirely different person!"

"Ok, so what do you want? Be clear!"

"I want her out of the picture. I want my wife gone!"

Even as he said it, Bryan couldn't believe those words came out of his mouth. His original intention was to ask for a job on Sonya Hartiq but now, right in the middle of the conversation, his mind did a one- eighty. His wife was rubbing his nose in things. With Sara out of the way, he could get it all back, including the kids. He could deal with that Sonya Bitch another time.

"Ok, so, you want your wife gone, right?"

"Yessir! And it has to be an accident. Otherwise, the cops will suspect me right away."

"We know how that all works Mr. Sam. Don't worry about it, and why did you bring just five Gs?

Didn't I tell you to bring ten thousand?"

"Uh, yessir. I'm sorry."

"Ok, we'll take care of it. You give all the info to my boys here. Wife's name, home address, where she works, boyfriend's name etc. we'll take it from there. Now, do you have that burner phone we called you on?"

"Yessir!"

"Give it to me."

Freddy took the sim card out and smashed the phone on the floor with his shoe. He threw the sim card over to one of the men sitting closest and told him to flush it down the toilet. Then he stood up out of the armchair and stared down at Bryan Robbins.

"Ok, I have to go. These guys will handle all the details"

Bryan held his hand out to shake Freddy's hand, but Freddy just turned and walked toward the door. As he grabbed the door handle to leave, he turned and said: "Uh . . . just one more thing. Who the hell is Bobby?"

"He's the guy in Omaha who told me to call you. Said you could help me."

"I don't like that. Give my boys his number too. We're gonna have a talk with this Bobby! And, when the job's done, you know what happens if you don't pay the other five Gs."

"Yessir! Don't worry, I'll have it all."

"I'm not worried pal. *You* worry if you don't have it."

CHAPTER 25

"To tell the truth"

M onday was a bad day for Ms. Sonya Hartiq. The Fairy Tale had come to an end. The carriage into a pumpkin, the glass slipper broken and thrown in the trash. She knew she'd asked Tony too many questions on the trip to Chicago.

"Who wants a girl friend who asks so many questions all the time?"

She really messed this one up. She was sure she'd seen the last of him. But, then, he gave her all that money.

"Was that his 'goodbye' gift? And what about the contracting job in Chicago? What was that all about? Maybe there was no job. Maybe he just needed an excuse to see me? I don't know."

It was all so strange. Yet, what an enchanting weekend. She'd do it all again in a heartbeat, Only, this time, she wouldn't be pushing him away asking so many stupid questions. He could have been the one. The Prince who would rescue her from the tower of obscurity, boredom and despair.

Tony's Monday wasn't much better. He was feeling bad about the way he and Sonya had parted. Freddy paid him the other $5k and expenses and an "Atta Boy" when he got back to KC; but money wasn't what was on his mind today.

His mind was dominated by thoughts of Sonya just as hers were on him. He was in a quandary. How could he tell her what he did in Chicago? What he did for a living. He whacked that guy sure as hell. But she felt so bad about the guy's supposed heart attack, how was he going to tell her that a heart attack had nothing to do with it.

And why did the mob call it "whacked" or "clipped" instead of "murdered," which is what it was. He guessed that was supposed to make whomever did the deed feel better about it. Was he a whacker or a clipper or a murderer? Wouldn't take Sherlock Holmes to figure that one out. How many dudes had he murdered?

No percentage in counting that. All he knew was that it got easier and he felt less guilt with each subsequent contract. The first one was tough. He sat with bad feelings and sleepless nights and regret for weeks. But, then came another job and another and that's what it was these days, just a job like any other. No different than going to work turning a wrench somewhere, except it paid better. He'd done so many in the past few years that he no longer felt any remorse. Chicago was just another gig. That guy had probably done the same thing to a dozen others. It was just his turn. So, when would **his** turn come? "Live by the sword, die by the sword."

"Whatever! Think about something else."

"Sonya!" He needed to call her. Maybe he could drive up and see her. That is, if she even wanted to see him at all. After the gun and the Mickey Mouse, Donald Duck phone call, she probably just thought he was crazy. But, he had nothing else going on this week. He'd call, and if she agreed to see him, he'd lay it all out on the table. Tell her who he really was and let the chips fall where they may. He started to call her several times; pushed most of the numbers for her phone but. kept hanging up before it rang on her end. He was afraid of her rejection. Still, he had to gather the courage to call. Maybe she'd be receptive. One more time:

"Hello!"

"Hi Sony! It's me! Tony!"

"Oh God Tony, I'm so glad you called! Are you ok?"

The relief he felt at that moment was indescribable.

"I'm fine Sony! Are *you* ok?"

"Yes! Well, no! But I'm better now that You called! After the way I acted in Chicago, I thought you were gone forever!"

"Damn! I thought *you* were gone forever! I miss you so much!

"Tony! Can you come and see me?"

"Absolutely! Tomorrow soon enough?"

"It's *not* soon enough, but hurry!"

"Ok! I love you! I'll see you tomorrow"

Sonya's reaction to his call was encouraging.

"Maybe he was over-thinking things. Maybe he could still save the relationship."

The next morning, he jumped in his Beemer and drove North to Omaha. The entire three-hour trip was spent practicing how he would tell Sonya about his *real* self. If he told her with just the right words and inflection, it might be ok.

"Well, maybe not OK but, maybe acceptable?"

He told Sonya he'd be there by noon and good to his word, he parked his car in the apartment complex at !!:50 a.m. Sony had been waiting, watching out the living room window for the past hour, just in case he came early. When she saw him in the parking lot, she immediately ran to the door. He wasn't even in the complex and it was swung wide open with a beaming Sonya Hartiq standing there, ready for the Hugs and Kisses Marathon. She literally jumped up on him, wrapping her legs around him, causing his overnight bag to drop to the floor. Moments later, they were inside, in deep, loving embrace.

After that, the entire day and evening was delicious. But Sonya sensed something was awry. Tony seemed troubled. There was an edge to his demeanor that she hadn't seen before. Finally, she decided to ask him if there was something wrong. Had he changed his mind about her?

"Sony, today, I love you more than ever. But, I have something to tell you about myself that may change your mind about me."

"Oh No! Tony please don't tell me you're married!"

"I wish it were that simple sweetie. It's many times worse than that, and after I tell you, I think you'll just want me to leave or worse."

"Oh my God! You're *engaged* to be married!"

"No Babe. Nothing like that. I don't even have a girlfriend. You're my girlfriend. This is different."

"Different?"

"Yes. Different like Mickey Mouse and Donald Duck and the gun you found on the bed"

"Well, now I'm really confused Tony. Talk to me. What's wrong?"

Tony sighed a long, frustrated, despairing sigh.

"Sony, you know when I told you I was a contractor?"

"Yes! Of course!"

"Well, I am. But not the kind I led you to believe"

"Ok"

Tony sighed a deep sigh again.

"Sony! I'm in the Kansas City Mob!"

"The Mob? You mean like the Sopranos?"

"Yes, only this is for real."

"For real how?"

"For real, like sometimes I'm a hit man"

"A hit man? You mean like in the movies where they kill people?"

Tony just looked at her and said nothing.

"You've killed people?"

Again, no answer.

"You've killed people! Oh my God! You *killed* someone in Chicago on our trip?"

Looking down, and down hearted, Tony slowly bobbed his head toward the floor and backup again.

"Oh my God! Oh MY God! No! This can't be true. Tony! Not you!"

After that, silence all around. They just stared at each other. Tears in her eyes and his were beginning to well up. He knew this was the end. No way she could handle this. The moments of silence felt like hours. Then...

"Tony! That money you gave me, where did it come from?"

"What do you mean?"

"I mean *where* did you get the five thousand dollars you gave me? Was that *blood money?*"

"No! It was just money!"

"Was it the money you were paid to kill that guy at that bar?"

Tony decided that this lie would be ok. No sense in pushing the issue.

"No Babe! I always carry a lot of cash with me. I've had that money for a long time. I knew you needed money. I love you. Simple as that!"

Now, tears were streaming down her face, sobbing. Her chest heaved, trying to catch her breath.

"Tony! Oh my God! I don't know what to do."

Again, silence.

"Ok! Ok! But it's not your *career* or anything right?"

Now she was making excuses for him. But, she knew better; she was grasping at any redeeming straw she could find. Anything to justify what the man she loved did for a living.

"Babe, you need to know that my own father was in the KC mob. I grew up around it. When he died I took his place; I had no other skills or education to speak of. But, don't spend my life running all over the place *clipping* people" (Tony couldn't bring himself to use the words 'killing' or 'murdering') "It happens infrequently, and by and large, these are bad guys. It's like war. Almost every one of them had rubbed out others themselves."

"Every one of them?"

That meant there were others.

"Did that guy in Chicago kill other people Tony?"

"Probably dozens. He was a bad dude."

"Well, how did you do it? I mean, you were with me the entire time except when you went to the bathroom. I never heard a gunshot!"

Silence again.

"Babe, if you want me to leave , I understand completely. I just can't say anything else."

Holding a soaked handkerchief in her hand Sonya looked at Tony through glassy, tear entrenched eyes and said:

"Babe, I'm going to need time to digest this. But, it's getting late. I don't want you to leave. Stay the night and we can sleep on it."

There would be no making love tonight. Small talk. Then off to bed. Neither slept very well. And, when morning finally came, you could cut the tension between them with a knife.

Tony decided to leave without fanfare. And, Sonya didn't make a move to impede his departure. They hardly spoke at all except as he was getting ready to walk out the door, he looked at her swollen teary eyes and said softly: "I love you." Sonya just stared without reciprocating.

No more to say. He left, closing the door behind him.

Sonya quickly ran to the living room window tearfully watching him walk across the parking lot. As he opened his car door, he glanced up at her window. She followed every move, as he pulled away and down the street. Then . . . he was gone.

CHAPTER 26

"Two of a Kind"

For Tony, the drive back home to KC was long and miserable.

"Why did I tell her? Everything was fine! She didn't really need to know. I should have kept my goddamned mouth shut. Why would you ever tell someone, anyone, you're in the mob, let alone, a hit man! It was stupid of me to think I could flower it up. She's gone. And, she ain't comin' back. I'm so goddamned stupid."

In Omaha, Sonya was crestfallen. The only man she ever loved turned out to be a murderer. How would a good Catholic girl from an Iowa farm rectify an issue like that?

"I wish he would have told me he was married or something. At least, that could somehow be resolved. If he loved me, he could get divorced. Happens all the time. But a murderer? You can't un-ring a bell! He didn't say how many people he'd killed but it had to be more than one. Come to think of it, he was probably the one who killed that guy at the Interlude. The paper said he had mob connections. What was he doing

in Omaha the weekend that guy was murdered? My God! What have I done? What has he done? And that five thousand dollars! I'm paying my bills with blood money!"

For days, terrible imaginings dominated every waking moment of Sonya's mind. Insomnia, then nightmares, then insomnia again. Through it all, she felt the pangs of the love she lost. Sonya still loved him, maybe now more than ever. Those continued feelings both confused her and enveloped her with guilt. How could she still be in love, now knowing who and what he was? But, of course, love's not a light switch. You can't just turn it on and off.

For his part, Tony tried to block the entire episode out of his mind. He went about his business in KC, banging heads and picking up the weekly "Vig" from the strip clubs and loan sharking. But, like Sonya, he was still in love. And, like her, he was confused about it. He'd been through a lot of women in his short life; but you could almost hear the glass crashing behind him as he walked away from one relationship after another. Not this time. But, he kept trying to resign himself to the idea that he would never see Sonya Hartiq again.

Weeks went by but the pain remained. Sonya began to rationalize.

"He said all the people he killed were bad guys didn't he? He never hurt anybody who wasn't a murderer himself. That's what he said! Is that so bad? That's why they have the death penalty. The State executes people all the time. Tony just gets the guys who haven't been caught. I know he'd never hurt an innocent person."

In fact, Tony once "Whacked" a female State Senator who was on the wrong side of a mob issue but, as they say: *"love is blind,"* and Sonya Hartiq wasn't seeing well these days.

The phone rings.

Tony Messina looks at the caller ID.

It's Sonya.

"Hello!"

"Tony! It's me! Sony!"

"I know! Sony, I'm so glad you called. I'm so sorry about everything."

"It doesn't matter anymore Tony. Not to me. I'm still in love with you and, if you still feel good about me, I want us to be together again. I can't stop thinking about you."

"I'm in the same place Sony. I've never stopped loving you. I know I'm just a piece of scum. I've done some bad things in my life and . . .

Sonya interrupted him.

"No! No Tony! I told you, it doesn't matter anymore. I love you unconditionally! That's how it's supposed to be isn't it? If you really love somebody, you don't put conditions on it. You are who you are. I may not love *what* you are, but I love *who* you are and that's all that matters. If you still love me, I'm ready to move on. I don't want to lose you."

All that morning, Sonya toyed with the idea of calling him. She just couldn't stand it anymore. Her thoughts fluttered back and forth, trying to decide if it was a good idea but, deep down, she knew she was going to do it. This fear of it all being over with him was madness.

"To hell with it! I'm going to call!"

"And, I never wanted to lose you either Babe! This is the best phone call of my life!"

The other phone line rings. It's Julian Infantino.

"Listen babe, I have to take this other call but, I'll get back to you later ok?"

"Ok Babe. I'm so glad I called you. Please call me when you can!"

Tony switched over to the other line.

"Hello Mr. Infantino! How can I help you?"

"Tony! I might have a job for you. Can you come down and meet me today?"

"Yessir! I'll be there by noon. Is that ok?"

"Perfect. See you then."

Julian Infantino wasn't a big one for long conversation. He hung up without a goodbye. His efficiency with words was legendary.

On the way to Julian's Tony had a stop to make. The phone call from Sonya had opened the door for him and he wasn't going to let it shut on him again. He was headed for TIVOL down on the Plaza. It's where all the Wise Guys went to buy gifts for their wives. If the wives didn't like what they purchased, they'd give it to their girlfriends.

Tony was on the hunt for a diamond. A *big* diamond. One he hoped she couldn't refuse. Sonya Hartiq wasn't getting away this time. She was going to be his wife.

CHAPTER 27

"One more time"

H e pulled up to Uncle Jimmy's right on time and walked back on the same creaky wooden floors to where Julian Infantino was sitting. This time, Julian sat alone. No henchmen around the table. This kind of business was best kept between two parties!

It was always the same when he arrived.

"Tony my boy! Come over here! Sit down!"

"Yessir Mr. Infantino. What's up Sir?"

"it's another one of Freddy's deals. Pays ten -large but we get our taste, which is half. Contractor pays the other five in person when the job's done. It's in Omaha."

"Omaha again? Hmm ... Ok, I'm interested."

Tony knew Julian always got a taste of any contract, and, since Freddy made the deal, he'd get his cut too. Five Gs wasn't really enough but, Omaha was just up the street three-and-a-half-hours, and it was an excuse to see Sonya again.

"Carlo! Get my boy Tony here a drink! What's your pleasure Tony?"

"A Bud Lite is fine sir"

Tony would have preferred a good wine, but Uncle Jimmy's wasn't exactly an upscale restaurant. Just an old bar and grill with a creaky wooden floor. Safer to just order beer.

"Sooo, what's going on in your life these days Tony?"

"Well, sir, I'm getting engaged."

"Engaged! To be married?"

"Yessir!"

"That's terrific! Just splendid! Is she Italian?"

"No sir, but I think she's Catholic!"

"You think? You don't know?"

"No sir, we haven't talked religion much."

"So, she lives here in Kansas City?"

"No sir, she's from Omaha."

"Omaha! Omaha! Hah! So that's why you want this project eh? Mix business with pleasure! Anyway, Congratulations my boy!"

"Thank you, sir! So, what's the deal on the contract?"

"Well, like I said, your end is five- large. Half now, the rest when the job's finished. Seems some guy wants his ex-wife to disappear. Freddy wrote out all the info on some paper here in this envelope, along with the down stroke. Also, there's some guy named "Bobby" who somehow got Freddy's number. Freddy don't like that. That guy's phone number is in there too. Freddy wants you to pay him a visit, find out how he got his number and how far he's spread it around. You know, just kind of feel him out and let him know he'd be smart to lose that number. Say! You want a sandwich?"

"No, thank you sir, I'm not real hungry. I'll take this info and head up to Omaha first thing tomorrow>"

"Ok Tony! And get me a picture of your girlfriend! I want to see who finally won the heart of Tony Messina."

Tony didn't look inside the envelope until he got to his car. It would have been considered rude to open it in front of the boss.

Inside, there were 25 one hundred-dollar bills along with a hand-written paper. There were no specific instructions, on the chance that the writings would be picked up by someone who might use it to incriminate the participants.

It was simply a list of information.

Sara Robbins, 11318 Davenport St., Omaha, Nebraska Housewife, 32 years old, 5' 3" tall. Blonde hair, green eyes, small woman, two children, boy and girl 5 and 7 years old, Omaha, Nebraska. Home most evenings. Goes out on weekends. Bobby phone number 402-555-7287 Bryan Robbins $2500 completed job retainer. Phone: 402 555-8884

This was all Tony Needed to do his work. He'd track her down when he got to town, follow her around a bit, and then do what needed to be done. He didn't like contracting for women, it felt primitive and distasteful. But someone was going to do the hit, and who was he to judge?

Again, he didn't want to drive his BMW in this venture. He rented a late model, black Buick Regal for the trip. He'd call Sony and ask if she'd like him to spend a few days with her.

Sonya had long ago set her cell phone to ring a certain way when Tony called, and when it did, she ran to the kitchen counter where she laid her phone to answer.

"Hello?"

"Hi Sony!"

"I'm so glad you called back! I was just thinking about you!"

"Nothing bad I hope!"

"Of course not! I miss you so much! When can I see you again?"

"Is tomorrow soon enough?"

"Yes! Yes! Hurry! What time will you be here?"

"I can be there sometime mid - afternoon. That work for you?"

"Sure! I'm looking but, I still don't have a job. I'm free! Hurry! Come to me! Hurry!"

"Ok Babe. I'll see you tomorrow, I have some errands to run now. Can't wait to see you!"

"Oh Tony! Please Hurry! I miss you so much!"

"Ok. Love you! Bye!"

Sonya had used most of the five thousand Tony gave her in Chicago to pay her bills. She still had about twelve-hundred-dollars left. She felt somewhat guilty about using it at first but, she still didn't have a job and, the "friendly" reminder statements were piling up. Tony would be back tomorrow. They'd work things out. All sins are forgiven.

CHAPTER 28

"Who's Knocking?"

The next day, Tony Messina jumps into a rented Buick with a two-and-a-half karat diamond ring sitting next to him on the passenger seat.

About 100 miles North of K.C. Tony he decides to get part of the job out of the way. He'd call this "Bobby" fellow and see what he was all about. He pulled out one of his burner phones:

"Hello?"

"Hello, is this Bobby?"

Bobby answered in a gruff voice.

"Yeah! Who's this?"

"My name's Tony. I have a question for you?"

"Whaddya want Tony?"

"I want to know where you got Freddy's phone number."

"Freddy? I don't know no Freddy. Bye!"

Just as he hung up the phone, Bobby realized that this was a call about the K.C. mob. Freddy was the mob connection. How did they get his number? He went into a small panic, looked at the caller ID on his phone and called right back. Tony answered.

"Hello?"

Bobby's tone was a lot more conciliatory.

"Uh hello there! Is this the Tony who just called me?"

"Yes. Is this Bobby?"

"Yessir! This is Bobby. How can I help you sir?"

"Well, Bobby, somehow you acquired a man named Freddy's phone number. Then you passed it on to someone else. Freddy doesn't like that you have his number. I need you to think about that."

Bobby's voice began to shake.

"Nothing to think about sir. I got his number from someone else who got it from someone else, but I don't need his number. I'll take it out of my phone right now! No problem!"

"That would be a good idea Bobby. Tell me, how many people did you pass this number on to?"

"Uh, just one sir. Just one. He called me and asked for it. I don't even remember his name."

"Well, Bobby, that guy called Freddy. Freddy doesn't like strangers calling him. He got really irritated, know what

I mean? Now, he has to change his number. He's kind of irritated that he had to go through all that. I'd like to suggest that you forget you ever heard the name Freddy. Sound good?"

Clearly shaken, Bobby's voice quivered.

"Yessir! I don't know no Freddy. Never heard of a Freddy and thank you for calling sir!"

"Ok Bobby. I hope I don't have to call you again."

"You won't sir. You won't. I don't know nothing about nobody!"

"Alright then, have a nice day."

"Yessir! Yessir! I will! Can I go now?"

"Yes, goodbye Bobby."

Bobby hung up, hands shaking.

"Damn! That Robbins guy! I TOLD him not to mention my name! He threw me under the bus!"

Two hours later Tony would be pulling his car into Sonya's apartment complex. He was excited about seeing her. He thought about calling her on the way but decided against it. He put the cruise control on, turned on the radio and listened to tunes.

Back in Omaha, Sonya was ebullient! Her lover was on his *way.* He'd be there soon.

Just then, there were several intense knocks on the door.

"Tony! He's here early!" Sonya ran to the door and swung it wide open!

Standing there with a sinister look on his face was one, Bryan Robbins.

"How you doin' Bitch? I just came by to remind you I know where you live."

With that, he simply turned around, walked away and down the stairs.

Bryan Robbins had been emboldened by his meeting with Freddy. The way he saw it, now that he actually put a contract out on someone, he was as good as in the mob; and he was going to project his new-found, dangerous self-image on anyone who crossed him.

Now, Sonya's ebullient attitude was nowhere to be found. In fact, she was scared out of her wits. His look was so menacing. The words he spoke came out in burning flamed whispers. She had never experienced something like that in her entire life. She wanted it to be just a bad dream but, of course it was real. It really happened. She was so scared. She reached over and gingerly closed the apartment door, turned the dead bolt and attached the chain guard.

Sometime later, another knock came to the door.

"Oh God! Please let this be Tony!"

Again, she ran to the door, but this time, she looked out the peep hole first. His face was partially covered by a bouquet of red roses but, this time, she could see it was her Prince.

"Yes! It's him! Thank God! It's him!

She turned the dead bolt, slid the door chain and opened the door as fast as her hands would allow. She jumped into him and wrapped her arms around his neck pushed the roses aside and began kissing him incessantly. Cheeks, lips, forehead, neck, everywhere. Sobbing into his shirt the whole time.

"Whoa! Hold on there, cowgirl!"

Tony was taken aback by her intense emotions.

"Babe! What's wrong?"

"Oh Tony! I'm so glad you're here!"

"I can see that honey, but something's wrong. Why are you crying? What's going on?"

"Tony a horrible thing happened to me today."

"Well, let's go inside. You can tell me all about it!"

Taking in deep breaths and sobbing, Sonya grabbed his hand, and led him inside the apartment.

"Alright, sweetheart, try to calm down. Tell me what happened."

"Oh Tony, you're going to think I'm some kind of awful slut!"

"My God Sony! What did you do?"

"Well, months ago, before I even met you, I had a one-night-stand with a married man! But I didn't know he was married Tony! Honest!"

"Well, ok. I guess you should know I'm not a virgin myself. Let's just forget about it, ok?"

"Tony! He came to see me today!"

"What do you mean? You had sex with him today?"

"No! No! Nothing like that! His wife found out about what we did, and she somehow got my phone number and contacted me."

"Ok!"

"You don't understand! She confronted me and I broke down and told her the whole story. It was just one-night Tony, and I didn't know he was married."

"I believe you Babe."

"Well, NOW, his wife is suing him for divorce."

"Ok."

"And he's blaming ME! He came to the apartment earlier today. I thought it was you. He stood at my door and threatened me. I thought he was going to hurt me Tony."

"Hmm ... seems like he and I have to chat."

"You're not mad at me? You don't think I'm a slut?"

"Of course not! There's no such thing as a slut. This is the 21st century! I never expected you were a virgin."

"Oh! Thank God!"

"Tony, don't you know by now that I'm hopelessly in love with you? Whatever you are, whatever you've done,

I have no control over how I feel. I don't sleep anymore. I stay awake in bed wondering where you are, what you're doing, if you're with someone else. Is he awake? Is he thinking of me?"

"Babe, I'm not as expressive as you are, but please know I'm going through the same motions. I've never known a woman like you. Here I am, a low life mobster, and somehow I'm asking you to overlook all that and be with me."

"I don't see you as a mobster Tony. I'll admit, when you first told me what you'd done, I was devastated. Heartbroken. But then I realized, I can't just turn off what I feel for you like a light switch. I'm so far gone in love with you, sometimes I can't breathe right. I shouldn't even be telling you this, but it would do me no good to try to hide it."

Sony, I'm not religious, but after our talk about Chicago I've prayed that you'd find a way to forgive me and call me.

With those words, they simultaneously leaned into each other's arms and embraced with the deepest passion. As they kissed, Sonya bit softly on his lips. That, and the warm exhale of the breath of her nostrils on his cheeks, aroused his manhood, and he softly pushed her backwards onto the couch. Now they would make love, more impassioned than all times before. Both consumed by the touch of the other. For this moment, they would become one. Sonya moaned with lascivious rapture, as his body shivered, comingling into her animated soul.

"Now, both sitting up on the sofa, it was almost spiritual. They had validated what they felt for each other. They were both caught in an inescapable web of love. Several moments passed before either said a word. Finally, with an awkward anticipation, Tony began to speak."

"Babe, I want you to love me, but you need to know who I truly am. It's not pretty. In fact, by now you know it's beyond horrible. I've killed people Sony. And not just that man in Chicago. I've done it several times. More than several, actually. And, I've done many other bad things as well."

"You don't understand Tony. It doesn't matter anymore. I know it *should* matter, but it doesn't. It did at first. I thought I was in some kind of bad dream. But it doesn't matter now. I think I know who you are. I don't condone it, but I've come to terms with it. I'm in love with you. Period."

"I'm in the mafia Sony. I'm a Made man. My father was a Made man. I followed in his footsteps."

"I'm in a Yoga club Tony. My mother took Yoga lessons. We're even."

"Whew! Ok then!"

Sonya took a sip of her wine.

"So! You plan on staying in the Mafia Tony? I mean, are you a Don or something?"

'No Babe. There's no such thing as a Don. I mean, there used to be back in the day and still somewhere in Sicily, but not in Kansas City. It's just the mob. There's a boss, and I work directly for him, but that's it. We had a restaurant here in Omaha some years ago. It was called Angle's. but it's gone now. As far as me staying in. I don't know anything else.

"You have any more scotch? This is delicious?"

"Sure do cowboy! Be right back!"

Sonya came back with the bottle and poured another into Tony's glass.

"Sony, let's push the coffee table away from the sofa, I want to do this right."

Sonya was confused. "Do this right? Do what right?"

Just as he said, Tony pushed the coffee table away from the sofa. He walked over to his overnight bag and pulled a small object out. Clutching it tightly in one hand, He walked back over to the sofa and in one motion got down on one knee in front of her.

Sonya was perplexed once more. "What kind of surprise does he have this time?"

He opened his hand to reveal a small, black velvet box. He opened it slowly to reveal a 2.65 carat princess cut diamond ring, throwing prisms of light all over the room.

"Sonya! I'm in love with you. I want you to be my wife. I'm asking you. Will you marry me?"

"Oh my God! Oh my God! Tony no! I mean yes! Yes, if you mean it. I mean Yes! Even if you don't mean it. Yes! Yes! Yes! I'll marry you! Oh my God!"

That pretty much settled it. She would have said "yes" in five different languages, just to make sure he knew what she meant.

"Babe, I wasn't sure coming up here just what to expect, but things have turned out just as I'd hoped. Then, Tony Messina slipped the jewel on Sonya Hartiq's finger.

For the first time in her life, thirty- two- year- old Sonya Hartiq was engaged to be married.

"Don't wake up! Don't wake up from this splendid dream! I have to catch my breath! I will not wake up! I refuse to waken! Why am I crying? Why is HE crying? Why are WE crying? Oh God let this be real! It's real isn't it? Isn't it real? "

Her arms instinctively grabbed the man kneeling in front of the sofa and held on like they were in a storm at sea and he was the only thing that could save her from the torrential wind and rain and yawning waves. And, in its own way. That was true.

As they both basked in the glow of the moment, Tony abruptly changed the subject.

"Babe, I'm gonna pay this Bryan guy a visit. You know how to get hold of him? His phone number. Where he lives?

"I have his phone number. His name is Bryan Robbins."

"Bryan Robbins. Ok. Where do I know that name from?

Then Tony had an epiphany, He pulled the note Freddy gave him out of his pocket and read the name of his contract mark again. There it was: Sara Robbins

"Sony! What's his wife's name?"

"Huh? Oh! It's Sara! Sara Robbins. Why? What's that got to do with it?"

Tony kept his face emotionless, but he was astonished. How could this be? This guy's wife was the same person he was hired to dispose. By now, Sonya knew what he did for a living, but he thought it wise not to rub her nose in it. He didn't want to tell her the other reason he drove up to Omaha. But, this was one weird coincidence.

"Well, give me his phone number. Me and Mr. Robbins are gonna have a sit down."

"You would do that for me Babe?"

"Hey! You're almost my wife! I'd do anything for you!"

In fact, Tony already had Bryan Robbins' contact information, but not wanting to divulge his other purpose for visiting Omaha, he decided to play dumb in that category. Tony had more on his mind than just talking to Bryan Robbins. This was getting complicated, and he knew how to fix it.

CHAPTER 29

"A Change of Plans"

Saturday, Sony was in the shower when Tony got the burner phone out and dialed up Bryan Robbins. It was unlikely that anyone would be listening to Mr. Robbins phone, but caution always ruled in these matters. At least on the caller's end it would be anonymous.

"Hello?"

"Is this Bryan?"

"Yes! Who's this?"

"Bryan, this is Carmine from Kansas City"

Even though he was on a burner, Tony didn't want to use even his first name, and Bryan wasn't sure what to think.

"I don't know any Carmine from Kansas City."

"I represent the company you hired to do the construction work on your upstairs bathroom."

Now, Bryan knew what the guy on the phone was talking about. "Pretty Slick" he thought.

"Oh! THAT Carmine! ! Yessir! How can I help you?"

"Well, I'm in Omaha now. We should have the job finished by tomorrow. If you're happy with the work, I'm supposed to meet with you to collect the balance.

"Oh! Ok! I have a room here at the Holiday Inn Express on 178th and Center, can we meet there?"

"Sure! As soon as the job's finished, I'll come over and collect the balance. What room are you in?"

"I'm in 217!. Second floor."

"Ok. See you soon. Bye now!"

Tony wasn't sure what to do. This Robbins guy had threatened Sony. In addition, he didn't like the idea of killing a woman; especially one with young children. He'd brought all the tools of his trade along with him, including the Soviet style handgun but, that wouldn't do him much good here. Whatever he chose to do, it had to look like an accident. A bullet to the head would immediately make the husband the first "person of interest." Plus, it wasn't that long ago he'd strangled *the* Coliano dude with a garotte right here in town. Another *"mob style"* killing and the police would start looking around more than usual. So, he wasn't sure just how to execute Sara Robbins. He'd brought syringes full of Fentanyl mixed with Heroine. No Carfentanil this time. It worked plenty fast, but it was dangerous even carrying it around in your pocket. Anyway, a Fentanyl-Heroine mix worked just as well, and he'd packed that along with some Ambien. Colorless, odorless and tasteless, you could pour it into a drink, put the person to sleep quickly, and then shoot them up with the Fentanyl-Heroine mixture. Voila! Drop Dead Lady! Who knew she was a drug addict? But he'd have to find a way to get next to her. He'd think about it.

Then, he hit on an idea. *"What if I took out the old man instead? If I got the cash, Julian probably wouldn't care who got clipped. Besides, it would eliminate the chances of the police interrogating the guy about his wife's death. If they did, he'd probably break sooner or later, throw all of us under the bus, and put the Feds right on our K.C. doorstep. And, it'll take care of his harassing my Sony. I think I'll drive over to the Holiday Inn right now."*

At that moment. Sonya came out of the bathroom in her robe.

"Whatcha doin Babe?"

"Uh . . . I've gotta put some gas in the car. It's almost on empty from the drive up here. . I'll be back in a little bit sweetie."

"Ok! Hurry! I miss you already!"

"Here you are Mr. Krasinski! Room 237, the elevator is just around that corner. The Breakfast Buffet starts at 6 a.m. sir!"

"Thank you very much."

Tony used yet another one of his many aliases. This time around: Ronald Krasinski. Like the Sanders identity, he had all the right documents: Driver's license, American Express card, the works. He also got the rental car from a different company. He'd taken an UBER to the airport and rented the car there. He was Anthony Sanders at Avis and Ronald Krasinski at Hertz

Looking around, Tony saw that there were video cameras outside the hotel and in the Lobby. When he went up to the room, he surveyed the second floor, making sure there were no video cameras in the hallway. It was clear. He would visit Mr. Robbins tomorrow morning.

While Tony was busy scoping out the hotel, Sonya made a phone call home

"Mom! It's Sony! Put Dad on the phone! I have exciting news!"

"What is it baby?"

"Just put Dad on the phone, I want to tell you together!"

"Ok hon! Sonya's mom yells out: "John! Pick up the phone! It's Sony!"

"Hello?"

"Dad! It's Sony. I couldn't wait to call and tell you. I just got engaged to be married!"

"Oh my God baby that's wonderful! Is it Robert?"

"No Daddy, Robert's long gone out of my life. His name is Tony!"

"Tony! Well, good! What does he do?"

"Uh . . . he's a contractor from Kansas City!"

Mom chimed in:

"A contractor! So, he's in construction! That's great honey! How old is this Tony?"

"He's 38 Mom! I just love him, and he loves me!"

"Well, obviously! We're both so happy for you! So! When's the wedding?"

"We haven't picked a date yet."

"Is he Catholic baby?"

"I don't know Daddy. We never talk religion, but he's Italian, so I'm guessing he's Catholic."

"Well, Catholic or not, you know the grandkids have to be raised Catholic!"

"Daddy, it's a little early for that. But don't worry, ok? You should see my engagement ring!"

Mom comes in again:

"Well, that was my next question. Did he give you a ring!"

"Oh mom! It's gorgeous! I can't wait to show it to you!"

"When do we get to meet him?"

"He's in Omaha right now! I was hoping you could drive down tomorrow and meet him!

Anyway, I wanted to tell you both right away! I'm so happy. Can you please make the trip?"

"I think so baby! John, can we drive down there tonight to meet Sony's fianc'e?"

"Absolutely! We'll see you in a couple hours sweetie"

"Ok Daddy! I can't wait for you to meet Tony"

They all hung up simultaneously. Sonya looked at the rock on her finger.

"My God! This must have cost him a fortune!"

Tony took Sonya out to dinner Friday night. As they left the apartment and walked to his car, she was perplexed.

"Tony! A Buick? What happened to your BMW?"

"It's in the shop Babe. Besides I don't like putting too many miles on it; easier to just rent a car. Are you embarrassed to be seen with me in a Buick?"

"Of course not! I just wondered. Tony, I have to tell you something. While you were out today I called my parents to tell them about our engagement. They're coming down tomorrow morning to meet you. Is that ok?"

"OK? That's terrific! I'd love to meet your parents. I'm really excited to meet my future in laws!"

While Tony really did want to meet Sonya's parents, he had other motives as well. He planned to take care of Bryan Robbins Saturday afternoon using the Fentanyl/heroine combination syringe. On the chance the cops figured out it wasn't a self- inflicted drug over-dose Sony might need an alibi. The first place they look for suspects is the spouse and then associates who might have a grudge. With her parents at her apartment, she'd be covered.

"Perfect! I can't wait to meet them!"

CHAPTER 30

"Mixing Business with Pleasure"

They woke by 8 a.m. Saturday morning. Sonya's parents would be there in a couple of hours. She had already cleaned the apartment anticipating Tony's visit, so there was nothing to do but eat breakfast and lounge around. They decided to eat at Denny's. There was one close up on 84th street near the interstate.

Just after they ordered, Tony excused himself to go to the restroom. No one else was there. A perfect time to call Bryan Robbins and give him directions.

"Hello?"

"Bryan! This is Carmine!"

"Yes Carmine!"

"The bathroom will be finished this morning. I'll have some pictures of the finished job to show you. You're going to love it. How about I come over to your hotel and collect the balance around 1 p.m. Will that work?"

Tony was talking in a bathroom stall. He could hear another guy walking in. It would be easy to listen in to the conversation, but It didn't much matter. After all, they were only discussing a bathroom remodeling.

"Sure! One o'clock! I'll be here. Just come up to my room."

"Ok! See you then!"

By the time Tony came back to the table, his breakfast had already arrived. *"just in time!"* he thought.

They got back to the apartment, beating Sonya's parents by just a few minutes.

There was the knock on the door.

"Surprise!"

While it wasn't really a surprise, the reunion of Mother, Father and Daughter was always a joyous event. Living an hour and a half away, Sonya's folks didn't get to see her that often. Tony stood right behind her smiling sheepishly as John and Marsha Hartiq entered the apartment.

Mrs. Hartiq was the first to greet him. "Oh! And you must be Tony! My gosh Sony! You picked a handsome one!" Sonya's father then reached over to shake hands. Hello, Tony, I'm John Hartiq"

If one hundred men were lined up and you were asked to "Pick out the hit man," most often, Tony Messina would likely be the last you'd choose. His entire demeanor was generally polite, reserved, and sophisticated. But underneath it all, if the situation demanded, he could be your worst, evil nightmare. Today called for the gentile, respectful Tony Messina, and he happily delivered.

"I'm so glad to finally meet you both! Here! Please sit down and relax, that's a long drive. Can we get you some coffee or something?"

John responded spontaneously. "I'll take a diet Pepsi if there's one in the fridge. Sony usually keeps a few in there for when we come by"

Marsha Hartiq spoke just as quickly: "Nothing for me, thank you! I'm just fine. I can't tell you how nice it is to meet my daughter's finac'e! Sony tells me you're in construction?"

"Well, yes ma'am! Sort of. I'm an independent contractor."

John Hartiq chimed in. "Oh! Sounds important!"

"Sony! Let me look at your ring! Look at this John! My God! It's gorgeous!"

Tony jumped in: "Thank you ma'am, I love your daughter very much and I wanted her ring to be something special."

Marsha looked up at her daughter. "Oh! 'Ma'am' he says! He's handsome AND polite! Where'd you find this guy sweetheart?"

"Well, mom, it was kind of by accident! In fact, literally by accident! I ran into the back of his car!."

"Really? And he didn't get mad?"

"No Ma'am. It wasn't her fault. I felt bad for her. She looked like she was getting ready to cry, so I hopped out of my rental car and tried to calm her down. After we moved the cars off the road, we had coffee across the street, and I guess the rest is history."

Now, John Hartiq spoke.

"Well, kudos to you young man. If it had been me, I'd have been pissing mad!"

The "getting to know you" conversation went on for a good hour and a half when Tony announced he had to meet a guy for a quick business lunch at 1 o'clock. It wouldn't take long, and he'd be back in no time. He winked at Sonya, indicating to her that he was going to meet up with Bryan Robbins and settle this thing once and for all. He excused himself with a "Be back in a little bit" and went out the door!

Driving over to the hotel, he had the Fentanyl syringe in his jacket pocket along with the Ambien and a bottle of Jack Daniels for the supposed celebration. On the way he called Bryan, just to make sure he was in his room.

"Bryan?"

"Yes!"

"Hello! This is Carmine! Your kitchen's done!"

Bryan wasn't sure how to react. *"Was this REALLY what he wanted? Was this a dream? Or did he really, actually do it. The mother of my children! God! Well, too late now."*

"Bryan, we're gonna need paid. I'm coming over right now. You have the money?

"Uh . . . yes! Yes! I have it right here. I'm in room 217!"

"Ok . . . I'm five minutes away. Stay off the phone. Don't call anyone. You can call your kids later if you like. I'll explain when I get there. Meanwhile, I have pictures for you. Your bathroom looks terrific! You're gonna love it. All in red!"

Of course, Tony had never done anything to Bryan's wife. But he didn't want him calling the house and her answering. He pulled up to the hotel and in less than a minute knocked on the door numbered 217.

"Bryan sort of crept up to the door. Half afraid to face the man who killed his wife. In a low tone, almost a whisper he looked out the peep hole, saw this man standing there, but was compelled to ask before opening.

"Hello! Who is it?"

"It's Carmine! Open the door!"

From the other side, Tony could hear the nervous shake in Bryan's voice"

"Sure! Sure!"

And there stood Tony Messina in all his glory. Bryan wasn't a small fellow. Almost six feet tall, not frumpy but married life and lots of alcohol had taken the chisel out of his physique. He stared at Tony for a moment. No fat on this dude. Anywhere. And he was handsome. Tall, dark and handsome. Maybe too handsome. He didn't look like what Bryan Robbins thought a "hit man" should be. Still, he had an intimidating presence.

"Well, you gonna let me in?"

"Yes, yes! Come on in."

"I brought some whiskey to calm your nerves, in case you need it"

"I could use a drink. Thank you! So, you really did it huh? You got it done?"

Bryan Robbins didn't want to use the words "You killed my wife" he just couldn't get that off his tongue. Instead he spoke in code. Words like "You really did it" and "got it done."

Meanwhile, Tony grabbed two glasses sitting on the hotel desk. With his back to Bryan Robbins he filled them with the liquor and poured the Ambien in to one..

OK! Here you go!"

"Thank you! I needed a drink. I never did anything like this before."

"You didn't do it, I did! Drink up!"

As Tony had hoped, Bryan drank the whiskey very fast. Hand shaking the whole time.

"Want another? I have some pictures to show you."

"You said that on the phone. You have pictures?"

Tony had no pictures, but he was pretty sure Bryan Robbins wouldn't want to see them anyway. This kind of thing was all new to him.

"Of course! We wouldn't expect you to pay for a bathroom project that wasn't completed!"

"No! No! I know you guys are square. Was it quick? Did you do it fast? Was there a lot of pain?"

"Well, Bryan, it was a tough job. And we had to be careful not to make any noise. Didn't want to wake the kids up. One of our people had a bad accident."

"An accident huh? Will he be alright."

"Actually, I don't think so. It's a she. She got hit during the demolition work. The only woman who works for us. Sadly, I don't think she'll survive. Hurt pretty bad. But you're not responsible for that. We have workman's compensation."

Bryan began to feel groggy. He'd whiffed down two whiskeys in record time. The one, loaded with Ambien. He flopped down on his bed. The idea of seeing the proof in pictures simply faded out of his mind and the conversation.

"Well, can we get paid Mr. Robbins?"

By now, Bryan was going in and out of consciousness. The Ambien combined with the whiskey had already begun to take its effect. He sprawled out on the bed, half awake, half asleep. He mumbled something barely clear enough to understand what he was saying.

"Uh . . . .ish in a top drawer a nightstand!"

Tony reached over and opened the drawer. There it was: Five thousand dollars wrapped in bands of a thousand. Looking back, he saw that Bryan had passed out. This was the moment Tony had hoped for.

Bryan Robbins was wearing a short sleeve polo shirt.

Tony pull out rubber tubing and tied it around Bryan Robbins bicep. Then, carefully pulled the Fentanyl/Heroine syringe out of this jacket and inserted the needle into Bryan Robbins' forearm. He pushed the plunger injecting the poison and let the syringe lie there stuck into Mr. Robbins forearm. He grabbed Bryan's right hand and placed it right next to his forearm and syringe. At that point, he then took a handkerchief out of his pocket and wiped off the entire syringe. In addition, he also cleaned the nightstand, the chair he was sitting in, and everything else he touched in the hotel room including the whiskey bottle which he would leave for the cops to find.

Not that it mattered. Over time, there had been hundreds of guests in this room. Fingerprints and DNA everywhere. Anyway, this simply looked like a classic overdose. Just then, Bryan's body shook a little, but that was to be expected. Probably death throes. Tony wiped down the glass that he poured Bryan's drink. Then, he grabbed his own glass, took it to the bathroom, washed and dried it, and set it back on the desk where he found it. There would only be one used glass. Then he grabbed the money, went to the door, and listened to see if anyone was in the hallway. Nothing. As he walked out, he wiped off the door handle inside and outside as well.

He walked casually to the second- floor elevator and even wiped down the elevator buttons inside and out, just to err on the side of caution. He didn't exit past the front lobby, but rather out one of the side doors so the front desk man wouldn't notice him walking by.

Now, back to the rental car and the short drive to Sonya's apartment where her parents were waiting for an exciting evening with Sonya and her husband to be. Total time, 96 minutes.

CHAPTER 31

"Dinner Time"

Dinner that evening was at Biaggi's. An Italian chain restaurant in Omaha that didn't look like a chain or have a chain style menu. The atmosphere was similar to something you would expect from an upscale Las Vegas hotel restaurant. Spacious. Earth tones. Ornate globe lighting hung from the ceilings. Crown molding, all accented by a huge fireplace situated on the far wall of the dining area. All this topped off with an extensive wine list.

Tony was impressed. Native Kansas Citians have always kind of looked down on Omaha for its pedestrian ways. It was generally thought of down south as a meat and potato town where farmer's hang out.

"This is really something Sony! How'd you find this place?"

Sonya's father added his approval as well.

"I'll say. Have you been here before Sweetie?"

"Oh Daddy! It's been here for years. I've come here lots of times. You have to try the Lobster Corn Chowder, it's to die for!"

"Speaking of dying" Tony thought. *"Mr.. "R" should be plenty dead by now. I wonder if they've found him yet?"*

Tony was sure the coroner would rule this a drug overdose, but Sonya, being with her parents all day at the apartment was a solid alibi in the event they suspected foul play. Generally, if a death is ruled a homicide, the first place they look is to the spouse or significant other, and then to friends and people who knew the victim. Most of the time, if it's a homicide, it turns out to be the spouse. Tony was confident Sarah Robbins had her own true alibi. So, *"All's well that ends well.* "though it didn't end well for Mr. Robbins.

No sooner had they been seated than Mrs. Hartiq started the interrogation.

"Sooo... have you two love birds picked a date?"

"Uh... no mom. It just happened a little bit ago. We haven't discussed that yet!"

"Ok! I just wondered when we might expect our first grandchild to arrive."

Mr. Hartiq chimed in: "That's enough Marsha! Give these two a break"

"I was just wondering John. You don't have to be so rude!"

With that, Sony changed the subject.

"So, Tony! How'd your business meeting go?"

"Hmm... not too well. The deal is dead."

Sonya was catching on.

"It's over?"

"Yeah, he doesn't want to bother with it anymore. Anyway, your mom's right! Let's talk about when and where we're going to be married."

With that, Marsha Hartiq lit up like a Christmas tree.

"Sony! I like your Tony more every time he speaks!"

"Thank you Mrs. Hartiq"

"Please! Call me Marsha! Or . . . 'Mom' if you like"

And that was how it went all through dinner. Everyone tried the Lobster Corn Chowder, which kept its promise of 'die for' delicious. Dinner was over by 7 and John and Marsha Hartiq decided to make the 90-minute drive back home that night, leaving Tony and Sonya alone together at her apartment. They were both beyond impressed with the nice young man who would soon be their son in law.

Once all of hugs and kisses and perfunctory 'goodbyes' were over, and mom and dad closed the door behind them, Sonya turned to Tony and asked:

"Tony! What did you do?"

"What do you mean Babe?"

"Did you talk to Bryan Robbins today?"

"Well, yes!"

"And what did he say?"

"He won't bother you anymore."

"He said that?"

"Not in so many words. But trust me, he won't ever bother you again. Babe, I know it's early, but I'm tired. It's been a long day. Can we get to bed early tonight?

"Sure Sweetie! And, I guess you know; my parents just love you!"

"Your mother's a hoot!"

"Yes, I'm so sorry Babe. She means well. She's just so happy for me."

"I really enjoyed her. Both of them actually. Your dad's a great guy! Thanks for having them over to meet me. So, our wedding is mid-September. I'm ready. I want you for my wife Sony."

"And I want you Tony. I want to be beside you forever."

The two of them slept well that night. They would make love again in the morning. Sonya was no longer on contraceptives. If they made a baby, so be it. They'd be married very soon, and there would never again be sex with strangers. They were committed to each other. And it was satisfying.

CHAPTER 32

"Not Again!"

Sunday Morning. 11:25 a.m., the doorbell rings at the home of Sara Robbins. Sarah is cleaning up the breakfast table.

"Who could that be? Probably Bryan, I don't hear from him all weekend, NOW he wants the kids?"

The doorbell rings again.

"I'm coming! I'm coming! Just hold your horses! What an asshole!"

Sara walked briskly to the front door, opened it wide, ready to chastise her soon to be ex, but instead, to her surprise, there were two uniformed policemen with serious stares. Her *demeanor instantly changed from irritation to concerned curiosity.*

"Hello" Ma'am, I'm officer Kinneck and this is officer Johnson. Are you Mrs. Bryan J. Robbins?"

"Well, for the time being, yes!" What's this about?"

"May we come in ma'am? We have some news about your husband>"

"News? What kind of news? What has he done now?

"May we please come in ma'am?"

"Well, ok. The house is kind of a mess, the kids have been playing. What's this about?"

She led them into the living room where they stood until she invited them to sit down, at which point they asked if she would do the same. The kids wandered in, which put a concerned look on the men's faces. Now she was worried.

"Mom! Why are the police mans here?"

"It's nothing baby, take your sister and go upstairs and play"

"But why are they here?"

"I said! Go upstairs and play, I'll tell you later!"

The children reluctantly left the room and headed for the upstairs.

"NOW! Why ARE you here?"

"Mrs. Robbins, I'm afraid we have bad news for you."

"Ok! What's that?"

"Ma'am, we found your husband dead this morning at the Holiday Inn Express on 178th and Center."

For a quick moment, Sara just stared. And then she started screaming horrifically.

"Oh my God! Oh my God! No! No! Oh my God! No! No!"

This brought the kids back downstairs.

"Mommy! What's wrong?"

Sara shouted over to them in a frantic voice. "I SAID go upstairs! Now!"

The two cops just sat there, both nervous as hell.

Divorcing the father of her children was one thing, but him dying was a whole other story. She couldn't imagine it!

"No! No! He's not dead! Tell me what happened! Tell me what happened! He's not dead. He can't be dead!"

"We're not sure ma'am, but it looks like he overdosed. Housekeeping found him in his room this morning."

"Overdosed! On what? Bryan doesn't do drugs!"

"That's all we know ma'am."

"Well, how did it happen?"

"I'm sorry Ma'am, we don't know anything, but they'll be doing an autopsy."

"An autopsy! Oh! My God! Bryan! What am I going to tell the kids?"

In fact, the kids heard the entire conversation. They went upstairs as they were told, but just far enough that Sara couldn't see them. Now, they ran down the stairs and jumped into their mother's arms crying.

"Mommy! Did Daddy die? Did daddy die?"

It was a tough thing to watch. The cops just wanted to get out of the house as fast as possible.

"I'm so sorry Ma'am! We have to go. Someone will be in touch very soon and give you details. Please excuse us now."

The cops had a "Let's get the hell out of here" look on their faces this time and left abruptly.

Tony hadn't left town yet. He and Sonya were having lunch at a small café when her cell phone rang. It was Jennifer.

"Babe, do you mind if I take this call? It's Jennifer! She never calls me on Sundays unless it's important"

"No! Go ahead. It's ok."

Tony was pretty sure what the call was about, but quickly decided not to interfere.

"Hello Jenn! What's up?"

"Sony are you sitting down?"

"Well, yes I am. What's up?"

"You're sure you're sitting down?"

"Yes! Yes! What's going on?"

"Stan just called me! Somebody died!"

"Somebody died? Who died?"

"Bryan Robbins died yesterday!"

"What!" Bryan Robbins? How can that be? He's dead?"

"Yep, Bryan's wife called Stan to tell him and Stan right away called me!

Listening to the conversation, Tony just sat there with his head down sipping his coffee. Sonya looked over at him in horror. She knew.

"Oh my God! How did it happen?"

"I don't know, they found him in his hotel room. Stan said they think it was a drug overdose."

"Drug overdose! I didn't think he did drugs!"

"Me either! Maybe the divorce pushed him into it! Anyway, he's gone now. I thought you'd want to know."

"Listen Jenn! Thanks for the call. I'm at lunch right now. Talk later ok?"

"OK girlfriend! Talk later! Bye!"

Sonya put down the phone, looking at Tony in disbelief. Tony had a blank stare on his face.

"Tony! What did you do?"

He just kept staring.

"What did you DO Tony?"

Tony mumbled softly.

"I can explain."

Then, in a loud voice, too loud for a restaurant, Sonya half shouted:

"Explain! How the hell can you explain this?"

"I will Sony, you'll understand when I tell you. Let's leave here and go back to the apartment."

Once in the car. Sonya started crying uncontrollably. "Tony! Oh God Tony! I thought you were just gonna TALK to him! I didn't want you to KILL him! The guy has two little kids! Oh my God! What did you do?"

As they reached the apartment, Sonya was still crying. Sobbing actually. She never liked the guy. To be sure, he scared her. Threatened her, gave her an STD, but he didn't have to KILL him!

Once in the door, Tony gently motioned for her to sit down on the sofa.

"Would you like a drink Babe?"

Still sobbing. "Sure! Make it a stiff one."

"Ok! I'm gonna tell you what happened. A contract came down from a man in Omaha who wanted his wife clipped."

"Clipped?"

"That means killed. Anyway, his wife was filing for divorce and apparently he couldn't deal with it and wanted her to be gone."

"And..."

"And, I got the contract. I'm not one for clipping women, but I know *somebody's* going to do it, so I take the deal since it's in Omaha and I get to see you. I just got the woman's name and contact information. I don't know who the guy is. When I get here, you tell me about this man, Bryan Robbins, who's threatening you! The name is familiar. I pull out the name of the mark and sure enough, it's this guy's wife! Well now, I've got a problem. I don't enjoy this kind of work, but as I said, I especially don't like having to clip a woman. So instead, now that I know who the payee is, I'll take care of him rather than his wife."

"Bryan Robbins *paid* to have his wife killed?"

"That's what I'm saying! He gave us half the money up front and I was supposed to pick up the balance when the job was finished."

"Wow"

Babe, if anyone else would have taken this job, his wife would be dead by now and he'd still be running around town living large"

"Oh my God Tony. What horrible things are happening?"

"I don't feel good about it Sony, believe me. But it is what it is. In the end, I saved Sara Robbins' life"

"Ok. Ok. I'll try to settle down."

Neither of them said much more. They just sat there in silence. Soon, Tony would have to head back to Kansas City and deal with Julian. The lovers kissed and hugged, and when she wasn't looking, he put a thousand dollars on the dining room table in an envelope. He knew she hadn't found a job yet, and really didn't want her to get one. Soon, they'd be married anyway.

CHAPTER 33

"Rational Lies"

S onya was in a conundrum. Finding herself between a rock and a hard place. She loved Tony so much, wanted to be his wife, have children. But now, it was clearer than ever; there was no question, Tony came from an unimaginably dark place.

Everyone had seen movies like the Godfather and The Sopranos about 'hit-men' and the mob. But it was hard to believe those people and places really existed. And here she was, engaged to be married to one and the same.

In the end, "love conquers all." Sonya began to rationalize about Tony's chosen career. She was becoming one with it.

"Like he said! He only 'clipped' bad guys! And Bryan Robbins paid someone to kill his wife! Tony actually did save Sara Robbins life! I could see why he had to do what he did! By taking out bad people he was saving the lives of others who they might have killed first. That makes perfect sense. My Tony wouldn't hurt anyone who didn't deserve it!"

And so, Sonya was now a convert.

"Tony my boy! Welcome home! How did things go in Omaha?"

"Everything went smoothly Mr. Infantino but, there was a catch."

"Catch? What kind of catch?"

"Well, you remember how that Bobby guy gave the contractor Freddy's number?"

"Kind of, yeah!

"Well, I talked to that Bobby dude, and it seems he wasn't very quiet about Freddy's number. I guess he was bragging all over town about how he had the direct line to the Kansas City mob!"

'That's no good! You shoulda whacked him! So! Did you get the job done? Get the cash!"

"Yessir! Here's the cash! I got the job done, but not the way it was set up!"

"What do you mean son?"

"Well, you know, the guy who set this up, got Freddy's number from that Bobby dude."

"Ok!"

"Well, things were looking pretty hinky. You know we don't like clipping women anyway."

"Go on."

"Well, when I called this "Bobby" he got really scared and spilled out the name of the guy who wanted his wife clipped. Turns out he was a real dirt bag himself. I figured if I clipped his wife, Bobby would know how it happened, even if I made it look like an accident. If the locals or the Feds got wind of it, they'd track this guy down and he'd give up Freddy and the rest of us in five fast minutes."

"So, what happened Tony?"

"So, what happened is I whacked the *guy* instead of his wife."

"What!"

"Yessir, I called him and told him we did our part and I was coming over to collect the money."

"So, he paid us to whack *him*?"

"Yessir! I got the cash and slipped a Mickey in his drink. Made it look like a drug overdose."

"Ohh, I don't think that's good Tony. If word gets around we don't fulfill our contracts..."

"Mr. Infantino let me ask you to look at this through another window. First, this wasn't a family hit. He was just some scum bag from Omaha who didn't like his wife. And, don't forget, we whacked Jerry C, up in Omaha just a few months ago. After the dust settles, the cops usually just chalk it up to a mob hit. "Oh well, nothing to do. But, If the cops suspected there's foul play so soon again, they might lose their sense of humor. Now, there isn't anybody to throw us under the bus! That Bobby dude was so scared when I called him, he started talking to himself. The only other connection to us was the husband. He's dead. Overdose! We got paid. Easy Peasey."

"You put it that way Tony, it makes sense. Here's your balance: Twenty-five- hundred cash."

"Thank you Mr. Infantino, I appreciate your understanding."

Say! While we're at it, I *do* have a job in New York. They came direct to me. A Wise Guy got sideways with the Calibris. He's an underboss. They want 'out of town talent' for this. If you don't want it, I can have Freddy handle it. He's got people. It pays twenty large.

"Twenty grand?"

"Yes."

"Expenses?"

No expenses. It's twenty large. You're in, you're out. One or two days. And, you don't even have to make it look like an accident. Calibris wants to send a message to anybody else who gets out of line."

"Ok, I'll do it. I appreciate the work sir."

"Good Boy! I'll tell Freddy. Here's the envelope with all the information. They want the job done by the end of next week."

Tony got up to leave and walk out when Julian asked . . .

"Say! Tony! One more thing! Did you get to see your girlfriend when you were up in Omaha?"

"Yessir! Got to meet her parents too! Getting married in September!"

"So soon! Congratulations! Hey! Here's some advice my papa told me when I was a young man: A new woman's like a new car. You're all excited the first couple months, then all you got's the payments!"

At that, Julian half laughed, half coughed an old man's cough at his own words.

Tony left feeling good about the meeting. Everybody got their money and Julian agreed with his Bryan Robbins switch. In the end, it was ironic and funny that Mr. Robbins unknowingly paid for his own execution.

Tony was apprehensive about calling Sony so soon after the last episode but, this was as good a time as any to find out if he'd lost her. Maybe she'd call off the engagement but, if she still wanted their relationship, such as it is, it was time for them to visit New York city.

Before Tony could get to his phone, Sonya called him to let him know all the details of what happened after Bryan Robbins death. On this call It was a whole different Sonya than he had known when he last left Omaha.

"Hello!"

"Hi Babe! Miss me?"

"I missed the hell out of you! ! You ok?

Sonya sounded happily excited.

"Sure! Except I miss you! I called to tell you the Bryan

Robbins story and to thank you for the money you so slyly put on the table. . Babe, you didn't have to do that, it's a lot of money and I'm ok! Honest!"

Tony was feeling very, very good now. It was as if the Bryan Robbins thing never happened.

"Well, Sony, I don't want you to get a job anyway, when we get married, I'd like you to move down here in K.C. You'll be my wife in a couple of months anyway, and you can find a job down here. Speaking of which, where do you want the wedding, here or in Omaha?"

"Whichever you want Tony, Las Vegas is ok with me. I'm just in love with you"

"Ok, we'll talk about it. Meanwhile, I'm heading for New York next week, I want you to come with me."

"Oh Tony! I would love that! I've never been to New York City!"

"Perfect! I'll drive up to Omaha and we'll both fly together from there. Sound good?"

"Sounds wonderful! Now, want to hear about Bryan Robbins?"

Sonya was being playful. Tony could hardly believe it.

"Yes, I do. That was sad that he passed. Was it a drug overdose?"

Obviously, they both knew what the deal was, but now they could speak in their own code.

"Yes! And guess what! He just happened to have a million-dollar life insurance policy! At first, the police weren't so sure there wasn't foul play, especially with her filing for divorce and all. But Sara had an airtight alibi. Then, I guess they decided it was maybe a drug overdose suicide. So, she's set for life! A million dollars tax free! She's just going to have him cremated. No memorial service, nothing. There doesn't seem to be many people who want to remember him anyway!"

"Hmm, but if it was ruled a suicide I don't think the insurance company will pay the claim."

"That's the catch! If a life insurance policy is two years old or older, it doesn't matter if the guy died by suicide or something else, the insurance company has to pay! I guess Bryan bought that policy back in 2012. And anyway, nobody's sure if it was accidental or not."

"Welp! All's well that ends well. I'll make the plane reservations tonight. I have some work to do down here, then we'll fly to New York on Sunday. Love you! Talk later sweetie."

After he hung up, it occurred to Tony was surer than ever that Sonya had accepted what he did for a living. The Bryan Robbins thing didn't seem to bother her at all. In fact, she was almost jubilant about it.

Surely, she knew damn well that if he had business in New York, what it would be about. He let out a big sigh of relief and satisfaction. Secrets were no longer necessary. And, if she was going to be his wife, he needed her acceptance of who he was and what he did.

CHAPTER 34

"Trip to Heaven, Road to Hell"

Sunday afternoon, 12:25, Tony and Sonya are on their way to New York. United Airlines, first class, Omaha to Newark. Tony knew the airport at Newark, was much less congested than JFK or La Guardia, New York and is just across the river. They'll arrive at 4:25 Eastern. Tony booked a suite at the Marriott Marquis right on Time square. Sonya was excited. She'd never been to New York City; she'd just seen Time Square on TV when they drop the ball.

Tony had a private limo waiting for them outside the airport terminal. The driver was standing at the baggage claim with the name "Sanders" written on it, so they'd know he was their connection ride. It was business as usual. "Mr. & Mrs. Sanders" had arrived.

It was a 45-minute drive from Newark International to the Marriott on Times Square, across the Hudson River on the George Washington into the city but, it all went very quickly for Sonya. New York City was like a fairy tale to her and every site and sound on the way was like candy and music to her eyes and ears.

This was glorious. The view from their room was glorious. For her, the moment was up there in the "Cinderella" category and the prince was right there beside her.

They spent Sunday downstairs at the hotel lounge, dining on gourmet appetizers. All day Monday were tourist things, dining at a quaint, almost hidden, Italian restaurant below street level, prime seating to the famous musical "Hamilton" at the Richard Rogers Theatre. Washington Square, even a comedy club in Greenwich Village. A whirlwind tour through the entire city.

Tuesday, Sonya was happily exhausted with the joy of her New York city experience. That's when Tony decided to ask Sonya to sit for a while. He had a request of her.

"Babe, I have some work to do here tomorrow night"

"Ok . . . I understand Tony."

"Well, it's kind of different this time."

"What do you mean Babe?"

"Well, there's a restaurant near Ozone Park in Queens called Don Peppe. They make the best baked clams and marinara in all New York. Anyway, It's a known hang out for Mafia types. You've heard of the famous Genovese crime family?"

"Well, yes!"

"Genovese capo Ciro Perrone used to hang out there"

"Ok"

"Well, there's a Wise Guy name of Tommy 'Shark Face' Bonnaci who got sideways with the Calibris family. They want hm clipped"

"He's a wise guy?"

"Honey, you ever see the movie "Good Fellas?" "Wise Guy" is a mob name like a "Good Fella""

"Oh! Ok! Well, what's that got to do with me.?"

"This Bonnaci Wise Guy will be at Don Peppe this Wednesday night. He loves the ladies. I need you to be there at the bar alone and let him warm up to you."

"Oh Tony! Honey! I don't know! I don't think I can do that!"

"I need you to do that Babe"

"Oh God! What if he doesn't like me? Doesn't hit on me."

"Don't' worry Babe, he will. You can wear something really sexy and act like you're on the make. I just need you to talk with him and invite him to your place. Just get him to go outside with you"

"And then what?"

"Then nothing, I'll come up from behind and take care of things"

"Tony, that makes me an accessory to ..."

"He's a bad dude Sony. He's probably murdered a dozen people himself. You won't even see him unless you turn around. I have a piece that makes no sound, no smoke, no flash, nothing. You won't even hear it, and neither will anyone else. Just keep walking and turn left, there's a grocery store right next door. I'll catch up with you. We'll call a taxi from the grocery store and come back here to the Marriott."

"Won't the cops know he was... clipped?" Sony was catching on to the mob's lingo.

"Yes, of course they'll know. But that's why we're here from Kansas City. The Calibris family wants to send a message. Bonacci was going to sing to the Feds. Nobody's going to track this down to someone from Kansas City.

"You mean a *couple* from Kansas City"

"Sony, all you'll do is walk a man outside who thinks he's going to get in your knickers, Ok? If you won't do it, I'll find someone else, some other way."

"No Tony! I'll do it. I'll do whatever you want. I love you. I know what your life's about. If I'm going to be your wife, I might as well know what's going on."

Tony sighed with relief.

"Ok Babe. Thank you! Things will go smoothly. I promise."

"I know. I trust you Babe. You know what you're doing." It came hard for her next sentence, but she got it out nervously: "You're a professional"

CHAPTER 35

"Partners in Crime"

The ride from Time Square to Ozone Park N.Y. is about 9 miles, a 37-minute drive on a normal day. That is, if Time Square ever has a normal day. Tony would tell the cabbie to go to 162 Lefferts Blvd. That particular address is a single-family home just 3 doors down from the Don Peppe restaurant. After the cab drops them off, the plan was for Sonya to walk ahead of Tony into the restaurant. Not good for them to be seen together. He would walk across the street to the 11th Avenue liquor store. While they were in the cab, Tony gave Sonya a picture of Tommy Bonnanci. Her job was to seek him out and sit next to him with her cell phone on and dialed into Tony's. Tony would hear when she lured him outside the restaurant, walk across the street, and do what had to be done. It should all be over by 7:30 or 8:00. Almost dark. A syringe killing would have been easier but, as the New York mob wanted everyone to know this was a mob "hit", it would be two shots to the head, right behind his ear with his hand-gun; known in the trade as the "Double Tap"

In her wildest dreams, Sonya had never imagined herself being in a situation like this; literally, a party to a murder.

But she rationalized what Tony had told her time and again. *"These were bad people, who had themselves murdered others. This was just saving the Great State of New York, the time, money and trouble of executing them.* Talking in a whisper so the cab driver couldn't eavesdrop, Tony kept assuring her that she was up to it and all would go well.

And so, the cab pulled up to the house, and the two partners in crime took their respective places. Tony crossed the street and walked to the liquor store. Sonya walked straight to the restaurant. She had memorized the picture of her intended victim and as she walked in, she spotted him immediately at the bar. This was good. Sitting at a table would have been more difficult. She dialed up Tony on his cell and walked up and sat right next to Mr. Tommy Bonnaci, appropriately named "Shark Face" as his nose stuck out like the dorsal fin of a shark and his eyes sort of bulged out of his skull. But he was dressed well, in expensive patterned silk shirt, dress slacks, Italian leather loafers, no socks. He was in deep conversation with another mobster looking type. "Birds of a feather." When Sonya sat down next to him, the conversation with the other man stopped abruptly. Tommy Bonnaci, turned to look at her. Sonya surprised herself by giving him a "Come Hither" smile. She certainly was dressed for the occasion. High fashion jeans, a loose satin blouse that revealed just enough cleavage to spur the imagination. A simple 14 k gold bracelet and red Rosana pumps sporting a leather ankle strap. Tony had picked out the entire outfit for her earlier in the day. Thankfully, the place wasn't too crowded. The fewer people who saw her walk out with him in tow, the better. But she'd have to separate him from his friend.

It didn't take very long for Mr. Bonnaci to start up with her. The smile she gave him opened the door for conversation.

"So, what brings you here tonight young lady?"

Trying not to appear as nervous as she was, Sonya replied.

"Oh, I just stopped in to get a drink after work. I just live down the road a way."

"You live in Ozone Park?"

"Well, yes! I work in the city, but I live here. You know how rent is in the city."

"Yes! I do. So! Can I buy you that drink?"

"If you like, that would be nice. I'll have a Manhattan"

Sonya, was playing this like she'd done it all her life. For his part, Tommy Bonnaci didn't miss a beat.

"Bartender! Get the young lady a Manhattan!"

Even before the drink got in front of her, he had already moved his bar chair a little closer.

"So then! What's your name?"

"I'm Amy! And can I ask who you are?"

"My name's Tommy, and my friend here is Buzzy"

Buzzy said nothing, but just leaned in on the bar and half waved his hand at Sonya.

"So, any plans for the night Amy?"

"Not really. I thought I might have some fun a little later"

Listening to their conversation on the phone, Tony could hardly believe Sonya was doing this well. He was almost getting jealous.

Tommy Bonnaci could hardly believe his luck.

"Well, if you don't have any ideas, maybe you'd like to hook up with me?"

"Well, what about your friend?"

"Oh! He doesn't care. Actually, we came here separately!"

Buzzy waved his hand again. Fact was, Buzzy was part of the whole set up. Sonya didn't know that, but Buzzy called Tommy to meet at the restaurant. Even Tony didn't know why Tommy would be there Wednesday night, he was just told where to go. No one said anything about a "Buzzy."

"Well, I'm parked outside. You want to follow me to my house?"

For Tommy Bonnaci, this was becoming too good to be true. But, he was hooked and ready to go. Sonya quickly slammed down the second Manhattan and got up off her bar stool, heading for the door. Tommy Bonnaci followed like a puppy dog.

Once outside the restaurant, she turned left and walked toward the grocery store as she was instructed. She could see Tony crossing the street, headed toward Mr. Bonnaci. She didn't want to look back. Tony caught up with them in a moment and she heard a dull "clack clack." Then she heard someone fall behind her. In that moment, her soul turned black. She had slid into the dark side. The next thing she knew, Tony was walking beside her as they both entered the grocery store, grabbed a cart and started shopping. In a few minutes, they called a cab to retrieve them. In the distance, they could hear police sirens approaching.

The taxi came to pick them up at the grocery store, and as they walked outside, on their right were several squad cars and a line of yellow police tape cordoning off the area. Tony asked the cab driver what happened.

"I don't know! I just got here! But with that yellow tape, it looks like a crime scene."

Sonya was shaking uncontrollably. There was no way out now. She was an accessory to murder. She had just joined the mob by osmosis. She vice gripped Tony's hand all the way to the hotel.

Neither said anything. Dead silence in the cab. She was still shaking as they entered their hotel room. Tony turned on the TV, and there it was. The entire crime scene enveloped by TV news camera trucks and police squad cars. A crowd had gathered outside, and she could see "Buzzy" standing there as a spectator. The whole experience had overwhelmed her. In complete silence, saying nothing, she walked into the bedroom, flung herself deep into a pillow and began to sob.

CHAPTER 36

"Going to the Chapel"

Tony came to her awhile later. Still in her clothes, Sonya had literally cried herself to sleep. Careful not to wake her, he crawled into bed beside her, put his arm around her, and took to sleeping himself.

The issue of eliminating Tommy "Shark Face" Bonnanci was not an unusual event in the life of Tony Messina. He had done this kind of thing more than a dozen times. Each assassination was easier the one before. But still, he remembered his first contract. Some "nobody" from Kansas City who got sideways with Carlo and the boys. He got the job done, but he was physically sick sometime afterwards. Now, his Sonya was feeling that exact pain. Even though she had not been physically involved in the actual slaying, she led the victim to his demise. Even being part of intentionally taking a life is an undertaking that permanently discolors your soul and manifests itself in physical distress as well.

But, the sun came up the next day as they both awakened almost simultaneously. As her eyes blinkingly opened, Sonya could see Tony sitting beside her on the bed, softly stroking her hair. The touch of his fingers was one of comfort and love. He whispered softly: *"Good Morning Sweetheart".*

For just a short moment, she wondered if yesterday was just a bad dream. But of course, it wasn't. It was all too real. As she sat up in bed, she asked: *"Are we leaving today Tony?"*

"Yes Babe, our plane leaves this afternoon."

"That's good, I need to get out of this city."

"I understand. Me too. Should I order breakfast? We have time."

"I don't know. I'm not very hungry Babe."

"I think we should eat Sony. I'll order breakfast with Mimosas. You go ahead and wash up. You've had a rough night.

"Ok Babe! But please don't turn on the TV, I don't want to see or hear what happened last night."

"Deal Now, let's get you up and into the shower. You'll feel better."

He was right. In a way, taking a shower felt like it had cleansed Sonya body and soul. She lingered under the soothing, warm water awhile; each droplet, enveloping her guilt and working its way down to the shower floor with an obliterating splash. She felt better. Ready for Breakfast.

When she came out to the living room area, she noticed, Tony's demeanor was especially tender. He spoke in a softer voice, looked at her with empathic eyes, touched her more lightly and tenderly. He knew what she was going through, and he would do his best to ease her pain and guilt and fear of what she may have become. He spoke to her in whispers.

"Well, here's breakfast sweetie! Let's sit down and try and eat something."

"Ok, Babe. I feel some better. Tony, I have to ask you something."

"Ok sweetheart. Talk to me."

"Tony, I want to get married."

"I know Babe, we're engaged, remember?"

"No Tony! I mean, I want to get married NOW!"

"Now? You mean today?"

"Not today, but that would be nice. But soon. Sooner than September. I want to fly to Las Vegas and be married. Next week if possible. Can we do that?"

"Yes! Of course! I'm just a little surprised. I thought you'd want a big church wedding"

"I thought about it. But I don't have that many friends or relatives. Just my parents really, and you've never mentioned a load of friends or relatives either. Las Vegas just makes sense. And right now, I NEED for you and me to be married. I NEED you beside me all the time Tony."

What was happening in Sonya's head goes back to primordial times. The need for protection. Someone to watch over her. For Sonya, the events of the past night underscored just how fragile life could be. It also reminded her how alone she was in the world. Her problems in life were all hers. Lived alone, unemployed, finances, scared at every knock on the door. To this point, Tony was just a part time visitor.

"Well, you're right Sony! Both my parents are deceased, and I have no real friends. Just associates really. My uncle Carlo has connections in Vegas. He can arrange something classy and special. This time next week, you'll be Mrs. Tony Messina. That is, if you want."

"Tony! It's ALL I want! Oh! Thank you Babe!"

Sonya, eyes welling with tears, jumped up from the dinette, knocked over the orange juice, wrapped her arms around Tony and smothered him with kisses. Cheeks, eyes, neck ears, forehead, everywhere. Today didn't seem so bad after all. Still, she didn't want the TV news turned on.

That afternoon, in the waiting area in the airport, Tony made a call to Julian Infantino. First, to let him know the job was done. The other reason was: Could Mr. Infantino possibly set up a wedding ceremony for next weekend somewhere on the Las Vegas Strip?

"Consider it done my boy! And, do I get to meet this young lady sometime soon?"

"Yessir! I'll bring her to K.C. with me when we get back."

"Perfect! I'll get hold of someone at Caesars today. Get you a minister and the biggest honeymoon suite in the place. My wedding gift to you! Will that work?"

"Yessir, that would be absolutely perfect. Could you see if we could have the ceremony sometime Friday afternoon?"

"I'm sure that won't be a problem Tony. I'll take care of it. You have a safe trip home."

"Thank you Julian! you're the best!"

For the first time in his life, Tony called Julian Infantino by his first name!

"Anything for you Tony, you know that. You're like a son to me."

Sonya was right beside Tony when he made the call. She could pretty much hear both sides of the conversation. She was overjoyed.

Twenty minutes later, they boarded the plane for Omaha, first class. Tony asked the flight attendant if they had any champagne on board. They did. Once the plane was airborne, they brought them both champagne and glasses. Tony and Sonya kissed and toasted each other to a life of endless love, romance and high adventure.

The trip back to Omaha went on without a hitch. Sonya was feeling better about everything. The champagne certainly helped, but it wasn't just that. Tony didn't speak a word about the night before, but Sonya once again rationalized that what they had done was simply eliminate a very bad person from the world, and in the process maybe save someone else from being smitten down the road somewhere. She was getting used to the idea.

Once landing in Omaha, they grabbed a taxi to Sonya's apartment just to check the mail. Probably just bills, but she needed to check on things anyway. After that they would drive to Kansas City and spend the week there. Sonya could leave her Toyota at the apartment for pick up some other time. This wasn't the time to drive separate vehicles.

They made it to K.C. early enough to enjoy dinner on the plaza and then headed back up to Tony's apartment. Jet lag and the three-hour drive from Omaha left them satiated. Nine o'clock. Time for bed. Sonya lived there now, with her almost husband. They pulled the covers up as she snuggled under her lover's arm. Tomorrow, she would meet Mr. Julian Infantino, head of the Kansas City Mob. All was right with the world.

CHAPTER 37

"Mr. & Mrs. Messina"

"So, this is the beautiful, soon to be Mrs Messina! What a beauty you are! You must be Italian, no?"

"Well sir, my mother's Italian but my father's Scotch, Irish"

"Well, that explains it! You take after your mother! Tony! You found a good one here!"

"Thank you sir!

"You know Sonya, me and Tony's father used to run together back in the day!"

"Yessir! Tony told me all the stories! Most of them anyway!"

"Well, there's lot of stories! Over the years, they get washed up a little, but most of them are true. So, I've got it all set up for you. Next Friday, 2 p.m. at Caesar's Palace, Las Vegas. The wedding chapel will have wall to wall flowers and the minister will be Monseigneur Gregory Thompson from Saint Anne's Catholic Church. He'll celebrate a Catholic wedding mass for you. Shouldn't take more than a half hour. If it's ok with you, I'll be there to help you two celebrate. I haven't been to Vegas in years.

They say it's changed now. Tony! I have something for you."

Julian handed him a thick, bulging envelope. It was the twenty thousand for the New York job.

As he handed it to Tony, he gave a glance at Sonya, not knowing if she had any idea what was going on. To put him at ease, she spoke up.

"Mr. Infantino..."

"Julian! Call me Julian!! Only Tony calls me Mister Agostina"

"Alright then, Mr. Infantino" Sonya couldn't bring herself to call him just Julian. He let it slide.

"I know Tony. I know what he does, and I love him. You don't have to worry about me. I was in New York with him."

"Well then, you just keep getting better and better young lady!"

"Thank you sir!"

"Well, ok then. Tony, you'll find an extra 5gs in there. Consider it a wedding gift. I'll see you at Caesar's next Friday. I promise not to get in the way."

With that, they said their goodbyes and walked out to the BMW. Once inside, Tony handed Sonya the envelope.

Sonya had never held that much cash in her hand before. She was speechless.

"You know, ten thousand of that's yours! Five for your help and five for the wedding present. We'll have a good time in Vegas."

Tony didn't want to elaborate on what 'your help' meant. He was sure she knew, but the idea was still fragile in her psyche. In the end, it didn't matter. Ten thousand dollars would buy her out of any credit card, car payment, rent problems she had. She never asked what kind of money Tony made, but she was sure it was plenty. He lived really well. Once they were married, she intended to ask in a very subtle way, but for now she'd just bask in the glow of all the wonderfulness surrounding her.

And so, the two of them partied the weekend away. Lunches and dinners at upscale restaurants all over the city. Nightclubs with live music. Back to the Green Lady Lounge for a jazz group called Al La Mode. Making love a half dozen times all the way to Sunday. Monday morning, they would drive up to Omaha and collect some of Sonya's things. She would follow Tony back to Kansas City in her Toyota and her new home in One Light Tower, Kansas City. On the way, she called her parents on her cell.

"Hello Mom!"

"Hi sweetie! How are you? How's Tony?"

"Mom, we're getting married this weekend in Las Vegas!"

"Oh my God! That's wonderful honey! Are we invited?"

"It'll be a Catholic wedding mom! Daddy can give me away!"

"Your father will be thrilled Sony! We're both so happy for you!"

"Ok mom! Please tell dad, I'll give you all the details later!"

"Alright honey. I can't wait to tell your father when he gets home!"

Sony could see Tony's BMW just in front of her. She dialed him up. They could talk on their cells the rest of the way to K.C. Life was good for Sonya Hartiq and Tony Messina.. They would be married in Las Vegas and honeymoon in Miami. Mr. Infantino had another job for Tony and, like before, Mrs. Messina would accompany him. Miami was perfect this time of year. Was she gaining weight? Just what was that little bump in her tummy?

The End